THE HIEROPHANT CARD

A Tarot Mystery

by

Bevan Atkinson

D1603433

© 2019 by Bevan Atkinson.
All rights reserved.
www.thetarotmysteries.com

Electra Enterprises of San Francisco

All characters and actions in this novel are products of
the author's imagination and are used fictitiously.
References to real people, events, establishments,
organizations, or locales are intended only to provide a
sense of authenticity, and are used fictitiously.

ISBN 978-0-9969425-6-0

Acknowledgements

My constant gratitude to Gentle Readers who encourage me to keep writing the damn book: Lyn Adelstein, Nancey Brackett, Tracy Blackwood, Judi Cooper Martin, and Hannah Mikles, who also serves as a preliminary editor. John Kremer is a marketing guru without whom I would have no terrific marketing slogan, and Lyn Adelstein is the one you want by your side doing the web and book design. She is also the cheerfully enthusiastic and capable marketing whiz at book fairs. David Young is exactly right for your manuscript editor. Yvonne Casey is an excellent RN. Debra Rodriguez, as always, provided invaluable expertise and is a stalwart friend.

Book Passage in Corte Madera and its sister stores in Sausalito and San Francisco foster fledgling writers in a profoundly effective way. Please buy books from those stores and from all of your local bookstores.

A grateful member of Mystery Writers of America, Sisters in Crime, and Left Coast Writers, I grow increasingly introverted as I ossify into this writer job, but look! I joined groups!

For

James Michael McGowan

Gone too soon, but Mike, that fervent contrarian, would probably disagree with such a judgment.

He loved a good listener.

We owe respect to the living; to the dead we owe only truth.
          — Voltaire

Listening is a magnetic and strange thing, a creative force. . . When we are listened to, it creates us, makes us unfold and expand.
          — Karl A. Menninger

We are like islands in the sea, separate on the surface but connected in the deep.
          — William James

≈⎮≈

The landline phone rang. It was a slow after-
noon. I'd already taken my long stroll along
Ocean Beach at the western perimeter of San
Francisco, and maybe I really did win a Rolls-
Royce and a free trip to Bali.

"Yolanda says you have to read my cards," a
woman said, as if she were annoyed by the idea.
Her voice reminded me of a band saw cutting a
steel plate.

"I live to obey Yolanda's every command," I
said, "but why don't you tell me who you are,
and we'll see where that takes us."

"Are you or are you not Xana Bard?" she said,
mispronouncing my nickname, "Zana" instead of
"Ex-Anna." My odd nickname comes from my
baby sister's inability to pronounce "Alexandra"

when we were kids.

"Not yet," I said.

"What?"

"Not until I know who's calling, please."

There was a pause.

I waited.

I heard her sigh, the sigh of a provoked and impatient person.

"Thalia Thalassos," she said, pronouncing her name "thuh-LEE-uh thuh-LASS-us. "I work with Yolanda."

I thought of the Muse of Comedy and decided to treat the call as a source of later hilarity when, over a lovely dinner at our favorite café, I would detail this conversation to my gargantuan and inscrutable sweetheart, Thorne Ardall. Thorne was currently away bodyguarding some ridiculously rich tech wizard who felt threatened by the world at large and was willing to pay Thorne's fee in cash. Thorne is always paid in cash, which cash he immediately converts into gold. Yes, gold.

"I see," I said to Thalia, not really seeing anything, but to encourage her to keep talking. "So why did Yolanda refer you to me?"

A Yolanda Jackson referral was in general a good referral. I've known Yoyo since we were in sixth grade, and I've done tarot card readings for many years, some of which Yolanda, a brilliant, meticulous CPA and tax attorney, has been the Querent for. In payment for the free readings she cooks up a giant pan of mac and cheese, which I then refuse to share. You wouldn't share it either.

"As if I knew why she would send me to you," Thalia said, still sounding annoyed. "She just told me I had to call and make an appointment. She told me you don't charge anything, which is good, 'cuz I'm stony broke right now."

"And yet, not knowing why you should take Yolanda's advice, you called me. So there's something going on that spurred you to do this."

The folks who ask me for a tarot reading are generally troubled by the commonest human concerns: love, money, work, health, family. If they've never had their cards read they're likely to be afraid of the unknown outcomes of the "fortune-telling" experience. But they don't see any other way to address the problem they're struggling with, so people like Thalia face down the ooga-booga reputation of the tarot and ask for help.

I heard another exasperated sigh.

"It's just..." she said. "Everything is a mess, and none of it is my fault."

Of course not.

"What sort of mess are we talking about?"

"Aren't you supposed to tell me? You're the psychic."

I held my temper. Yoyo had referred her, and Thalia's life was a mess, and I'm the adult child of alcoholics — in other words, Codependents 'R Us.

I basically can't resist diving right in to fix every-one and everything except me.

"You haven't had your cards read before, have you?" I said.

"God no. Never. All those storefronts with neon palms lit up and all I see is how much rent those scam artists pay for their retail space using money from suckers who are too stupid to figure things out for themselves."

"Of course. Well, you'll be thrilled to see how little neon my card readings entail."

"What? What are you talking about?"

"Thalia, when I read cards for someone it's a partnership. We work together to figure out what's going on and what would be the best way for you to proceed. You will not be asked to cross my palm with silver, nor am I going to say you'll meet a dark stranger on a long sea voyage, unless you've already signed up for a cruise to Namibia. When we're done, if we've done our job well, you'll feel both recognized and released, instead of feeling lost or hopeless or whatever you're feeling now."

"Huh."

I waited. I never offer to set up an appoint-ment, because that step belongs to the Querent. People who discover that I read tarot cards will often say, "I'd love to have a reading," or "Would you read my cards?" and I always say yes. Then I wait for them to ask, "When can we do it?" and they almost never do.

I think they stop short because reading someone's cards means that to some extent I'm invading the Querent's private life, so I leave it to the Querent to say something like, "Are you free next Monday?" If they feel like they can trust me, they ask. If not, they don't. I'm fine with either outcome.

"How soon can we get together?" Thalia said, taking the necessary step. "Yolanda says the sooner the better."

"That's up to you. My schedule is pretty open."

My schedule is open because I don't have a day job. I used to have a Director-level title at a tech startup, and I was excellent at Directoring, and then a new COO came on board who wanted me gone so she could commandeer my budget, the end result of which was a massive legal settlement in my favor, followed not long ago by my father's death and an inheritance.

So I live in my comfortable house next to the Pacific Ocean with a significant, some would say excessive, number of pets and an unusual and unusually sizeable cash-to-gold-converting boyfriend, my downstairs cavalier.

Thalia made an appointment for the next afternoon. I called Yolanda to find out what the hell was going on with the lady who had pretty much all of Bullfinch's and Edith Hamilton's Greek mythology books bundled into her name.

"I should let her tell you," Yoyo said. "But my personal assessment is that she's screwed up to the max, which she didn't used to be. She's basically a good person, and until recently she'd been a solid and reliable help around the office, which I would like to see her revert to, so thank you for taking this on. I owe you a sizeable shipment of mac and cheese."

Okay then.

≈2≈

Bryce Gilbertson ambled down the polished gray linoleum hallway toward room 404. Alert to any late-visitor sounds from the curtained rooms he passed, he brushed his right arm along his hip, confirming that the syringe was tucked into the pocket of his loose-fitting, cornflower-blue scrubs. He loved the crisp detergent aroma of the cotton. So clean-smelling, unlike the patients and even some of the nurses. He loved that every day he came to work there was a row of industrially laundered scrubs waiting for the staff in the locker rooms.

The thick synthetic rubber soles of his work shoes made almost no noise as he walked. He placed his feet carefully to avoid any linoleum squeaks as his feet flexed.

It was five minutes to five a.m., almost the end of Bryce's shift, and the hospital floor was silent. Visitors and treating physicians were not yet arriving for the day and only a skeleton night staff remained on duty. His shift tasks during the night had been routine: assistance with changing adult diapers, administering meds, repositioning unconscious patients to prevent bedsores, taking and charting patients' vitals, the standard duties. There were long idle stretches between rounds.

He stopped just short of the door to the dimly lit semiprivate room and looked around to be sure no one was watching. Lifting his left hand to his ear, he probed the interior gently with the long nail of his pinky finger. Yes, there was dried wax almost the same color as his pale skin to pry away and flick onto the linoleum.

Bryce stepped inside room 404 and looked around to be sure that since the last time he'd checked on the current patient no new patient had been moved into the second bed beyond the separation curtain.

No.

Which meant Mr. Khouri was alone and asleep, so the timing was perfect. Mr. Khouri had been admitted two days ago, so the autopsy that would have been mandated if he'd been admitted within the last twenty-four hours was no longer likely. Bryce eased the syringe out of his pocket and moved soundlessly to Mr. Khouri's bedside.

≈**3**≈

Thalia's Mediterranean olive-tone face, when I opened the front door to her, was heavily made up. Her dark eyes, lavender eye-shadowed and painted with a wide, arched swoop of black cat's-eye eyeliner, sported thick black false lashes. Glossy cerise lipstick capped a look that went out in the 80s, if it was ever in on any day except October 31st.

Wavy hickory-brown hair with bleached highlights fell down her back onto a black cotton-poly knit hoody. Blue jeans slashed at the knees stretched tightly around her considerable curves, and lilac nail polish glinted at the open toes of her perforated black suede booties. She stood maybe five-foot-three without the boots' platforms and tapered stacked heels, and with them she was still

a few inches shorter than I am. She carried a battered tan leather hobo purse slung over her
shoulder. Her long, square-edged acrylic nails
matched her toenail color.

"You live here all by yourself?" Thalia said as
she turned sideways to slide past me and walk up
the stairs to my front hall and living room. She
hadn't bothered to wait for me to invite her in,
and her question was an accusation.

I followed her upstairs, smelling a dense miasma of patchouli. Why would anyone who is not
an actual farmer or a hunting dog want to reek of
wet dirt?

I had put the freshly bathed dogs, big black
Hawk and little brindle Kinsey, out in the side
yard dog run so they wouldn't rush my visitor
with that demented skitter-everywhere energy
just-bathed dogs exhibit. The black cats, Meeka
and Katana, had bolted upstairs and cowered under the nearest bed as soon as the doorbell rang.

Thalia stood in the hall, staring into the liv-
ing/dining room and upstairs to the third floor.
The fragrance of crushed mint leaves that I'd
hoped would impress my guest favorably was
overwhelmed by patchouli.

"Wow," she said. "This is all yours?"

"I have a tenant who lives on the ground
floor," I said to Thalia's back, thinking of Thorne
as my gold-loving Id in the basement.

"Yeah, but still, you have all this space, and

that view."

She pointed through the French doors to the Pacific Ocean beyond my fenced Japanese garden. She walked toward the view and then turned to peer around the wall into the kitchen. The east kitchen windows look onto 48th Avenue, and the north windows face the eucalyptus trees, cypresses, and Monterey and Norfolk Island pines that thrive in Sutro Park.

"Jeez," she said. "Some people have all the luck." She shook her head. "At least it's clean. A place this big, I don't know how you can keep it clean. And a white kitchen, too. If I had that color cabinets they'd be disgusting in about two minutes."

I thought of my housekeeper, and of my mother, referred to by her offspring as "Mater," but never to her face. Mater's watchwords are: "We have people who *do* that sort of thing."

"So where do we go? Here?" Thalia pointed to the dining table.

"Hi Thalia," I said, holding out my hand. "I'm Xana Bard."

"Oh, okay," she said, putting her hand into mine, gripping hard and letting go. Her skin felt like a scrub pad. She made momentary eye contact and then glanced back at the view, the living room, the view again.

"What can I get you? Water? Tea? Coffee? Soft drink?"

I neglected to offer Thorazine or a bong hit, which may have been a hostess oversight, given her visible jumpiness.

"It's not a social call, for Chrissake. Can't we just do it?"

She rummaged in her hobo bag. I prayed it wasn't for cigarettes. Nope. Cinnamon sugar-free chewing gum. She unwrapped the gum, looked around for somewhere other than back in her purse for the wrapper, and I held out my hand for it, like a Mom.

"The reading will probably work better if you're comfortable. It's a little chilly today, so how about some tea?"

I am extremely competent at making tea. Dumping dry leaves into a container and dousing them with boiling water represents pretty much the extent of my culinary talents.

"If I have to," she said, shrugging past the "thank you" part of the exchange.

"How about chamomile? Or whatever you like. Come with me and take your pick."

I dropped the gum wrapper into the trash bin, and opened the pantry door. I pointed at the tea selection, which took up three shelves and cov-ered the alphabet from Assam to Yunnan. Black, green, hibiscus, jasmine, rose hip, all of those and their many cousins were represented in multi-colored boxes and metal canisters.

"Oh for Chrissake," she said. "How am I supposed to pick from all these? Don't you have Lipton or something like real people drink?"

"Why don't I pick one for you?" I said, counting to ten as I filled the electric kettle and plugged it in.

The hiss and turmoil of immediate heating caught Thalia's attention as I pulled out a box and removed a chamomile tea bag, unwrapping and stretching out the label on its stapled thread. The soft floral aroma of the flowers reassured me that there were ways to defeat patchouli.

I gave Thalia a tea bag rather than loose leaves because I thought a real pot of tea would confound her.

"Is the water boiling already?" she said, listening to the kettle's activity.

"In just a moment it will be. Pick a mug, why don't you?"

I pointed to the cupboard where mugs lived.

"It's not going to be as complicated as picking the tea, is it?"

"Would you like lemon? Milk? Honey? Turbinado sugar?"

"Oh for Chrissake. Dump a goddam Xanax in there, why don't you?"

And she laughed. I looked at her and smiled, and she laughed harder, until tears pooled and she began to sob.

I unplugged the kettle, put my arm around Thalia's shoulders, snagged a box of tissues from the island countertop and steered her out of the kitchen to the living room sofa. I kept my arm around her and handed her tissues, waiting patiently for her to cry herself out. I held off swabbing her entire body down in an attempt to erase the off-putting reek of swamp mud.

Strangers who come to me for a reading are often frightened, and fear can convert all of us into self-centered, fight-or-flight-stricken impalas watching the cheetah coil itself for an eruption into a high-speed hunt.

When Thalia regained control, I took my arm from around her and put the tissue box on the coffee table.

"Well," she said, shaking her head and mopping up her bloodshot eyes and reddened nose, "that was fucking embarrassing."

"But necessary," I said.

For the first time, Thalia looked me in the eye and held the look. Her mascara had raccooned and her false eyelashes had come unmoored at the edges.

"Yeah," she said.

"Want to tell me why?"

"Oh why not?" Thalia said. "Somebody tried to kill my husband and the cops think it was me."

≈4≈

I finished making the tea and brought the steaming mugful of calming chamomile to Thalia. Crossing to the bookcase I opened a sandalwood box and pulled out my silk-wrapped deck of tarot cards. Unveiling the cards, I spread multiple scarves on the coffee table and began shuffling the deck. The spice smell of the sandalwood clung to the scarves.

Tarot decks are often larger rectangles than the cards we play Hearts and Go Fish with, plus there are roughly fifty percent more cards in the tarot than we use for modern card games, so it can take practice to shuffle them adroitly. I've been reading cards for many years and I'm still not an adroit shuffler.

"I'm just warming them up," I told Thalia.

"They get cold sitting in the box. I mean the actual temperature, not anything metaphorical. I'm just manipulating them for a while to bring their temperature up."

Thalia watched my hands and nodded.

"In a few moments I'm going to give you the cards, and you can shuffle them until you feel like they're ready."

"How will I know?"

"You just will."

She lowered her mug toward a silk scarf.

"Could you use a coaster, please? The scarves are only for the cards."

"Already with the woo-woo," she said, reaching for a coaster. "Why are the scarves so sacred?"

"It's a long tarot tradition," I said. "For me, the cards deserve special treatment because of the gift they are to me, and to the people who ask them for help. So I, like many readers, give my cards a silk wrapper to live in."

I felt the cards reach body temperature and held them out to Thalia.

"Shuffle them any way you like until you feel like they're ready."

"Can I look at them?"

"Sure. Whatever feels right."

She tried to shuffle them the way you do playing cards, but a clump slipped out of her hands onto the table. She scooped them back together and, rather than try to shuffle in the "normal" fashion, she spread the 78-card deck out onto the scarves and began smooshing them around. A card upended itself and flipped: the Hierophant, or Pope, card. She turned it back over without looking at it and continued smooshing.

I notice when a card calls attention to itself. Well, I mean, I know the cards don't have independent agency, but when a card flips over or falls out of the deck face up I've found it invariably has relevance to the reading. The same card will usually show up in the subsequent layout, or I might ask about it and explain its meaning and the Querent will be startled by the importance of the information the renegade card conveys.

As Thalia continued smooshing, I prayed the silent invocation I always pray before a reading: that I might allow light to pass through me without refraction or distortion, for the benefit of both of us.

Thalia pulled the cards together and stacked them.

"I feel like they're done," she said.

I let the stacked cards sit while I waited for the urge to do something with them. I don't use a consistent layout or formula for readings; I lay out the cards in a format that feels right at the time.

I put my hand on the deck and slid the cards sideways, spreading them across the scarf in a broad horizontal array.

"Pick three," I said.

Thalia pulled three cards, leaving them face down in a row. I turned them over; from left to right were the Queen of Swords, the Hierophant reversed (upside down), and the Seven of Wands.

Well, she said she didn't murder her husband, so at least for now I would take her word for it, no matter what the cards had just announced.

≈5≈

"Ugh," Thalia said, pointing at the Queen of Swords.

If there is a card to say "Ugh" about, the Queen of Swords is certainly a candidate. There are countless tarot deck designs, in all of which the Queen of Swords can be counted on to be stern and forbidding, one arm wielding a battle sword. In the deck I read she holds not only the sword; in her other hand she clutches a severed head by the hair.

She's a widow by intention.

"One of her nicknames is 'The Widowmaker,'" I said. "We'll talk some more about her in a moment."

I wanted to focus on the Hierophant, who had shown up in the center of the cards Thalia pulled.

That he was reversed gave a twist to his usual meaning.

"Thalia, you drew two Minor Arcana or suit cards, the Queen of Swords and the Seven of Wands. In the cards you play Bridge or Crazy Eights with the Swords are now called Spades and the Wands are Clubs. So the Queen of Swords is now called the Queen of Spades."

"The Old Maid," said Thalia.

"Exactly. Or the worst card to get in Hearts. The Queen of Swords has some serious overtones that resonate to this day."

Thalia thought about that. She pointed to the Seven of Wands.

"And this one?"

"You can see from the man holding up a long stick to fight off six people attacking him with their own sticks that the card is about conflict," I said. "So at its most obvious meaning, your cards are describing a situation in which you are alone, in conflict with multiple other people."

"Holy shit," she said.

She looked at me, her eyebrows lifted, so I went on. I wanted to talk about the Hierophant and how he was the crux of the matter, and that the other two cards flanking him were out-growths of his presence. I flipped the Hierophant upright so Thalia could read the title at the bottom.

"The card in the center is the powerhouse of

the reading," I said. "He's one of the twenty-two Major Arcana, which are a big deal. The Major Arcana are separate from the suit cards, and they carry more weight. That he's in the center means we have to give him special attention. Plus he's reversed here, which changes his interpretation a little."

"He looks like a judgmental old bastard."

I reminded myself that the cards are just little pieces of cardboard with colorful images on them, and there is never any need to defend my two-dimensional guides. They'll take care of themselves just fine.

"When the Hierophant is right-side up he can be strict. His other name is the Pope, and he can be interpreted as traditional religion and morals, your judgmental old bastard as you called him. But I look at the imagery and I see the repetition of threes in his miter and staff and robe. I think they refer to the integration of our physical, mental, and spiritual selves.

"When the Hierophant is reversed, as he is here, what I get from the card is a need for social approval, a looking to others for guidance, rather than confidence in your own strength of character. And more than that, to me this card is all about listening to our own inner voice, our own conscience or higher power — whatever you want to call it. When we listen to the external voices that try to boss us around, we lose our sense of who we really are as an integrated whole self. We may ignore our better angels, if you will, and that can allow us to blame everybody else instead of taking responsibility for our situation."

"Bullshit." Thalia was scowling. "I'm not responsible for the fact that my husband was cheating on me with a home-wrecking whore. I'm not responsible for the fact that he's lying there all banged up and in a coma after being thrown from his horse Buddy at the Tevis Cup. I'm not responsible for the police treating me like a criminal."

I waited until the bloom of anger drained from her face. There's no sense in trying to reason with someone whose emotions are temporarily in charge. I made a mental note to find out what the Tevis Cup was.

"What *are* you responsible for?" I asked.

"What do you mean?"

"Just what I said. What do you take responsibility for in your current situation? The Hierophant reversed can mean that you're not listening to your inner voice, the voice that tells you the truth even when you don't want to hear it."

"I have a lot of unpleasant inner voices, and they yell at me all the damn time. I get so frustrated I just want to drink a bottle of wine, eat a pint of butter pecan ice cream, and forget everything."

"What do the voices yell at you?"

"Oh God, everything. I'm fat and I wear too much makeup and I have no taste in clothes and I shouldn't eat that carrot cake. Also my husband is a loser and a fuckwit and I never should have married him because I'm going to wind up alone and broke and homeless."

"Ah. Okay then. Well, the inner voice the Hierophant represents is not the voice that says things like that to you."

"Then what is it?"

"The inner voice I'm talking about is the voice that's always kind. Always helpful. Always suggesting that you do the right thing."

"I don't think I have that one. Not that I've noticed, anyway."

"Hence the Hierophant card in your reading. He's a reminder that all of us need to cultivate our trust in ourselves by listening to and heeding that kind, helpful voice. Call it your conscience. Jiminy Cricket. If all you're hearing internally is criticism and reproach, I'm going to suggest some ways of peacefully shutting those voices down and promoting the nicer one."

"But that can't be why I needed to get this tarot reading. My real problem is my marriage that's gone to hell. Oh yeah, and this supposed attempted murder of my husband that the cops are on my ass about. Because they think somebody pushed him off his precious Arab gelding that costs more than our mortgage to feed and shoe and saddle and stable. And is still costing me even though Don can't ride him or his other horses now, or maybe ever again."

I pointed at the Hierophant card to bring Thalia's attention back to him.

"The willingness to seek and develop that inner voice is the central message of this reading. The Hierophant flipped over while you were shuffling, and now he's front and center in the three cards you pulled. But let's talk about the other two cards, because my guess is they relate to the problems you're trying to resolve."

"Please. Because that inner voice crap is just more woo-woo."

My experience has taught me that tarot readings give you the message you need to hear whether you think you were asking for it or not, but I let Thalia steer the topic away to the other cards. It's fruitless to try to hammer a nail of insight into a cast-iron ingot of resistance.

"The Queen of Swords is about the conscious choice to be separate, especially by using verbal attacks to maintain distance. She doesn't allow emotions or creativity or hard physical work to blunt whatever hurtful things she can hurl at the people around her."

"What you mean is, she doesn't put up with other people's bullshit."

I took a deep cleansing breath and let it out slowly.

"What I mean is, using harsh words to others leaves damage in its wake. No apologies can fully heal the scars cruel words carve into the affection people may have felt for you before you said them."

"You have to be tough in this world, to take the crap life deals out to you. 'Sticks and stones may break my bones, but words will never hurt me.'"

"I can see that you've got a lot of very difficult stuff you're dealing with right now, and you're doing your best to cope and be strong in the best way you know how. If only the 'sticks and stones' saying were true after we graduate from the playground. Because that saying is a brave way to face down a playground bully, but the truth is, words can indeed wound us in lasting ways."

"No matter what you say, my husband made a vow to be faithful. We've been married for over twenty years, and he's been cheating for at least the last year with the town bike. I just found out that the first time he and that homewrecker Jenny did the deed was on my birthday last year. Can you believe it? Anyway, I'm going to get a divorce and make him pay and pay and pay for what he's done."

I pointed at the Seven of Wands card.

"Who's resisting you?"

"Everybody. My kids are unhappy. They're grown and on their own, so at least they're not being exposed to all this except from a distance. His whore girlfriend, believe it or not, is against the divorce too. She's married herself, with no plan to get divorced or give up the affair either. She says she's just a wild child and can't see why anybody should be upset about something as simple as sex.

"The fuckwit wants to know why we can't all get over it and be friends. He wants to keep living in our house and keep his girlfriend on the side, as if I'm the crazy one to think that's not okay. And I've told the neighbors, who are my friends, and they've told more neighbors, so now Don and Jenny are mad that everybody is shunning them. Most of the neighbors are on my side, which the fuckwit thinks is 'so unfair.'

"Meanwhile, I have to make all these medical decisions about his care when the truth is, all I really want him to do is die. Oh, and the whore has been visiting him, and some of the nursing staff told me she's pretending she's his wife. A couple of times she's even contradicted my orders about his care. It's just a big fat mess."

Well, I had to admit she had a point.

Thalia's eyes had pooled with tears again. I pulled the box of tissues toward her and she snatched one out of the box and smashed it to her nostrils.

"We were really happy for a long time," she said. "Until he started with the horses and met the homewrecker. Now it's like I don't know what I ever saw in him."

And then she shook her head and waved her hand in a gesture I read as "Oh, whatever."

Shakespeare wrote, "Sweet are the uses of adversity." I'm pretty sure he was being sarcastic. I don't think Thalia was feeling any sweetness in her adversity at this point.

When she made eye contact with me I said, "How are you feeling about this experience right now?"

She heaved a sigh and shook her head again.

"I feel like I've talked about this situation to my friends until I'm blue in the face, and now I've talked to you, and it makes no difference. Shit still goes on being shitty."

"What do you want to have happen? And, if I may make a suggestion, see if you can ask your inner voice for what will result in the best possible outcome for everyone involved, rather than just badness for everyone except you. See what your inner voice can come up with."

"Are you serious?"

"I couldn't be more serious. After all, what has constantly chewing this same depressing cud of bitterness and resentment gotten you? Why not try another approach and see what happens?"

"You *are* serious. I knew the woo-woo was never going to let up if I did this."

"We be woo-woo. Woo-woo be us," I said, smiling.

"Oh for Chrissake. If I thought you really understood what was going on, I might maybe take some of your advice. But I don't believe you have a goddam clue."

Well, fair enough. I'd only known Thalia for an unpleasant hour or so. What did I care whether she took my advice?

But she was suffering, and meddlesome me was reading Thalia's cards and failing to make a dent in her impenetrable resistance to free-of-charge woo-woo wisdom.

"What are you doing tomorrow?" I said. "We'll hang out and you can acquaint me with what's going on so that I can maybe get something like a goddam clue. After which, maybe I can offer some helpful information. Information that's practical, and not all infected with woo-woo."

I shrugged, indicating that it was up to her.

She looked at me out of her wrecked eye makeup, narrowing her reddened eyes and judging how much to trust me.

She must have been pretty desperate — desperate enough to risk some trust. She gave me her address and told me to be at her house in the Oakland hills at nine o'clock the next morning.

≈ð≈

I heard the downstairs doors open and close. The sound was almost undetectable, which meant Thorne Cadogan Ardall, the mighty stealth-meister, was home. I felt the shimmering sizzle his presence always evokes in me, maybe because we maintain separate dwelling spaces in the same building and I'm never sure whether he's down-stairs in his apartment, or that he'll want to climb upstairs for a visitation. Since it's my house and he's my Sweetie, I can invite myself downstairs too. He and I are cooperative that way.

If Thorne adhered to his custom, he'd take a shower and change clothes before texting to ask if I was interested in a visitation on the back deck.

I'm perennially interested in having Thorne visit on the back deck, but I love that he checks first rather than assumes that his sizzle effect continues to make him welcome.

I made tea—mint for me and orange pekoe with honey for him—and brought the mugs out to the deck. I took a deep breath of the salty tidal ocean smells sweeping up the cliffside.

I felt an atmospheric shift when Thorne opened the French doors and stepped outside to join me. As silent as he is, nevertheless it's tough for the atmosphere not to shift when a six-foot-eight, two-hundred-sixty-pound human makes a move in your vicinity.

He kissed the top of my head and lowered himself gingerly, as he always lowered himself gingerly around anything not made of tempered steel or granite, into the Adirondack chair next to mine. His thatch of blond hair was damp-combed back from his face, but would fall over his forehead as it dried. Holding our warm tea mugs we watched the ocean and listened to the cool afternoon breeze ruffling the leaves in Sutro Park.

"What's the client situation?" I asked.

"Paid off."

Thorne meant that he himself had been paid off and no longer had a client. Thorne himself is not a payer-offer.

"Is there more to the story?"

"Moved to Macao."

"And the money bin?"

"Plumper," he said.

Thorne's money bin, where he keeps the gold wafers and coins that he buys with the cash, and only cash, that his clients pay him, has grown steadily plumper since I've known him. No disability insurance deductions, income tax withholding, social security, etc., for my off-the-grid thug swain. He prefers the reliability of shiny precious metal and shuns on-the-grid-triggered junk mail.

"Do you have another client?"

He shook his head no.

"Are you up for hearing about my latest venture in futzing around with someone else's less-than-ideal existence?"

He turned to look at me, five o'clock shadow darkening his sunburned ivory skin. He was wearing gold-mirrored shades, but I'm pretty sure he crossed his eyes before he nodded once.

"This woman named Thalia, referred by YoYo, came over for a reading. It was eventful, as card readings go."

"Mac and cheese?"

"Absolutely."

Thorne held out his mug toward me. I realized we were toasting the imminent arrival of mac and cheese, and we clinked mugs. Thorne doesn't mind that I like to meddle with other humans, especially if a Yolanda-generated high-carb casserole was the payoff.

It was my meddling that brought us together in the first place, and Thorne seems okay with my

ongoing urge to investigate and maybe occasion-
ally solve other people's problems. Not that he's
ever said anything. Thorne doesn't generally say
anything.

"What do you know about horse races?" I
asked. "Specifically the Tevis Cup?"

I've ridden horses on and off since I was a
child, and recently I'd worked with draft horses
on a farm, but the Tevis Cup was new to me.

"One hundred miles in twenty-four hours.
Grueling. Dusty. Half the riders don't finish."

"Do people get injured?"

"And horses."

"How would anyone know if you were
pushed off your horse instead of falling?"

Thorne shrugged. "Witnesses? The rider?"

"The rider who was pushed is in a coma."

Thorne shrugged again. "The horse?"

I hadn't asked about the horse. Trust Thorne
to worry about the horse, since he examines every
situation from all angles. I drew a conclusion
from Thalia's grousing that Buddy the Arab gelding was not injured.

"Stabled and eating, so probably okay."

Thorne nodded.

"DeLeon," he said.

"Why?"

I have no objection to calling DeLeon; he is the
world's coolest human and always a pleasure to
encounter. I just didn't see the link with what

Thorne and I were discussing.

"Maxine and Netta ride."

"Seriously?"

DeLeon and his family live in Piedmont, a wealthy East-Bay suburb, and they are African-American.

Thorne gave me a look.

"Oops," I said. "That was some presumptuous racist shit I just popped out with, wasn't it?"

Thorne turned his gaze back to the ocean. We watched the ocean and listened to the trees until the now-cold afternoon breeze drove us indoors.

Thorne grilled some chicken and vegetables. I love that he's the primary chef in our household, but it's also just as well that he take charge if we plan to consume edible food.

Dinner was yummy, and later so was he.

≈⫟≈

"Hi DeLeon. It's Xana."

"Hey there, Ms. X. How you doin?"

DeLeon Davies can speak English like a litera-ture don at Oxford if he feels like it. When speaking with me he rarely feels like it.

"It's all good at this end, my friend. I have a question for you if you've got a second."

"I'm between pickups at SFO, so hit me."

DeLeon owns a car service. Even in a ride-sharing hot spot like San Francisco his clients remain loyal, because he's DeLeon. Holding well-informed conversations with his clients has allowed DeLeon to invest wisely during the multi-decade tech boom; hence, the Piedmont house, complete with view and swimming pool. Also, apparently, complete with horses.

"Thorne tells me that Maxine and Netta ride horses."

"They do that."

"I'm wondering where they stable them, and if they know the Thalassos family."

"There's only the one nearby stable, up the hill across Highway 13. And yeah, they know Don and Thalia."

His tone registered a whiff of disapproval. Only a whiff, though, because DeLeon is steadfastly neutral about folks who don't cross the line into some form of unmistakable rudeness.

"Do you know if Maxine is free to talk? Or Netta, if she's around?"

"Maxine's home cookin' somethin' too good to miss out on. Why don't you and your boo come on over tonight and you'll see what I'm talkin' about. You can ask her and Netta what you need to know."

That was DeLeon. No questions about why I needed to find out about the Thalassoses, no worries that Maxine wouldn't make enough food for last-minute guests, just unspoken trust that his friend needed help and he would do what it took to provide it, and that Maxine would be unruffled if the entire Seventh Army plus buglers showed up.

≈𝟪≈

Maxine, her skin the color of polished mahogany, had baked four chickens after stuffing them with lemon slices and fresh rosemary. There were French-fried sweet potatoes, greens, biscuits, and then peach cobbler with vanilla ice cream afterward. DeLeon, whose face was the color of shelled pecans, was bartender.

During dinner we chatted about how the Davies' kids were doing. Their son Terrell would graduate from Stanford next Spring with a degree in electrical engineering; their oldest daughter NAME THIS OLDER DAUGHTER XXXXwas up for partner in a small San Francisco law firm that specialized in intellectual property law; their youngest daughter Netta was about to enter her senior year in high school, doing well after a frightening episode with a cult.

Sitting out on their patio, all of us stuffed with great food while we watched the sun set over the Golden Gate, I asked about Don and Thalia Thalassos.

Maxine shook her head and blew air out of her nostrils.

"What do you want to know, Xana?"

"Anything you can tell me. I'm not sure if you've heard about his accident."

"Everybody at the barn has heard about his 'accident.'"

"Maxine, are you saying you think there might be something fishy about that?"

"Girl, everybody who knows those two thinks there was something fishy about it. Thalia comes up to the barn all the time raising holy hell about her husband and Jenny carrying on with each other, saying she's going to beat Jenny's ass if she doesn't let Don alone. Nobody likes Don much; he's always yelling at the kids who come up to take their riding lessons. Nobody likes Jenny much either. Don's not the first married man she's gone after. And his isn't the first marriage Jenny's wrecked, either. Some of the mothers are talking about writing a letter to the Park Service that operates the barn, trying to get those two banned. Netta says the boy, Jenny's son, talks about doing something to stop the affair. She said Kyle caught Don and Jenny going at it one time. Can you imagine?"

"Yuk. That poor kid."

"Truly. Anyway, at some point a couple of years back Don got all wrapped up in long-distance races."

"The Tevis Cup?"

"Like that. He bought extra horses and a big truck and horse trailer and he goes all over to these weekend events. Then he decided he could be a coach and get people to pay him for learning how to ride those races. That's how he got involved with Jenny and her son."

"Did he do well in the races?"

"Well enough to finish most of them. Never a win or close to a win, that I heard of anyway. And I would have heard. Everybody talks to each other up at the barn."

"Any evidence of Thalia or anyone else acting out toward Don or Jenny?"

"I heard Don yelling one time about his helmet, about sabotage or some shit, but I just ignored him. He was always fussing about something."

Maxine sent us home with peach cobbler. We would have to provide our own ice cream. We didn't quibble.

40   The Hierophant Card   ר

≈𝓆≈

At the beginning of his next shift Bryce waited with the other staff while the charge nurse went over the night's new and ongoing cases and impending duties. The cleaning crew was moving through the floor, leaving a miasma of pine cleaner and bleach smells behind them.

When a new patient was named as having moved into room 404 Bryce waited to see if anyone would ask about Mr. Khouri. When no one did, he dared the question, but only after asking about two other patients who had been moved off the floor. He already knew they'd been discharged as scheduled, but he pretended he didn't and let Philippa, the charge nurse, confirm that the patients had been released.

"And Mr. Khouri?" he said after Philippa finished.

"Mr. Khouri passed away this morning."

"Ah. That's too bad. It seemed like he was do-ing okay."

Philippa looked down at her computer screen. "He was stable, but the attending decided the DVT had broken loose and the patient died of a PE."

Bryce understood the acronyms. DVT was a deep vein thrombosis, or blood clot. PE meant a pulmonary embolism, which was a blood clot blocking the lung; the clot prevented the lung from oxygenating blood and recirculating it to the heart. A pulmonary or cardiac embolism almost always caused unpreventable death.

Every medical professional knew that the big danger of a DVT was that it would break loose from wherever it started out and travel to the heart or lungs. Mr. Khouri had been in the hospi-tal being monitored and dosed with IV Heparin to try to shrink and destroy the clot, but the doctor and nurses accepted without question that the clot had broken loose and caused the patient's death. Bryce knew they would accept the likely PE, because deaths like Mr. Khouri's happened all the time.

The nursing team knew very well that nobody who occupied a hospital room in these days of health insurance strictures and limitations was in anything but very poor health; the risk of patient death was a constant, and so was the occurrence of death.

Bryce relied on the frequency of explainable deaths, and so far so good. Mr. Khouri had been a complainer, a real jerk, cursing Bryce when all Bryce was doing was taking his vitals. No family members visited Mr. Khouri—no surprise—and the world was better off without him.

The team's daily orientation continued, and at last Philippa asked if there were any questions. When no one had any, the nurses and support staff moved away to start the night shift.

Bryce had his eye on the ICH patient in room 412. Intracerebral hemorrhages, ICHs, were unpredictable. The man had had a terrible riding accident. He hadn't been wearing his helmet, the idiot, and had come in with compound fractures as well as the severe head injury. He had been unconscious when admitted and had undergone immediate surgery to relieve the pressure on his brain, and was in an induced coma now.

Bryce liked to stand at the foot of the patient's bed, watching his bruised and motionless face and listening to his ventilator-assisted breathing. This patient was young enough to be an ideal potential organ donor.

His accident was just tragic, and completely avoidable, so it was his own fault for doing something as dangerous as riding a horse that outweighed him five times over. But he still had the chance to do a lot of good for others.

Bryce lifted his pinky to his ear, exploring for dried wax to excavate and flick away. He began to plan.

ר   ר   ר

Changing out of his street clothes at his anti-septically scoured one-bedroom apartment three blocks from the hospital, Bryce thought back to the moment during his previous shift when he'd feared his time was up. He'd walked into the ICH patient's room, checked for anyone watching, and then proceeded to work with the support person to shift the patient's pillows and bedding so that the man was in a slightly changed position. He couldn't be moved too drastically because of his broken limbs. The two staff members had cleaned up the patient and changed his gown. Bryce had then excused the other man, saying he could take the patient's vitals without extra help.

These tasks complete, Bryce thought the coast was entirely clear. He slid his hand into his pocket for the syringe.

A toilet flushed behind the closed bathroom door.

"Who are you?" he demanded of the woman who opened the door. He felt his face burning in a blush.

"I'm his wife," the woman said.

"I don't think so. We've been alerted about you. Your name is Janey or Jenny or something.

You're not a permitted family member and you are here long after visiting hours have ended. I'm calling Security."

He knew he was overreacting as a result of his panic, but it was done and he couldn't scale back his threat now. Bryce reached up with his left hand for his communication mic to alert the desk and summon a guard.

"Please," Jenny whined. "We're in love, and I need to see him. I know he knows I'm here and it's helping him get better."

This patient is never going to recover, Bryce thought.

"Why are you smiling that way?" Jenny said. "Like a smirk. Like you know he's not going to get better."

"He has severe injuries. Recovery will be very challenging."

"But you say that like you don't believe it's possible. I thought nurses had to always think positive or something."

"Ma'am, are you going to leave voluntarily or do I have to summon a guard to escort you from the hospital?"

"What's your name?"

"Bruce J-Jones."

Damn. That stammer as he shifted the hard "G" of Gilbertson to the soft "J" of Jones.

Jenny snatched at the laminated badge hanging on Bryce's chest, turning it over to see the name. He pulled his right hand out of his pocket to grab her wrist and the syringe came with the hand, falling to the floor with a clatter and rolling under the bed.

"You're lying. Why are you lying about your name? And what's that thing for?" She pointed to where the syringe had rolled under the bed. "I'm going to report you."

Their voices had risen. Philippa, the night team leader, appeared in the doorway.

Philippa took charge, summoned a guard, got the protesting stowaway visitor removed, and everything went back to normal. But Philippa had given Bryce a look when Jenny mentioned the fake name he'd used and then demanded to know what the syringe was for, pointing under the bed where it was lying out of sight.

Yes, that had been a close call.

Thank God Philippa had followed the guard out with Jenny. Bryce had had a moment to grab the syringe and chuck it into the used-sharps container. It was normal to carry around a syringe, because nurses regularly flush every patient's IV port with saline, but Bryce didn't want that particular syringe's contents verified.

It might be time to start checking out the job possibilities elsewhere, Bryce thought maybe Portland or Seattle would be worth looking at. Always better to jump ship too early rather than too late.

≈*10*≈

Thalia and I sat staring at the unconscious man in the fourth-floor room at St. Joseph's hospital. His left leg was elevated and in a cast, as was his left arm. His head was bandaged and what facial skin we could see was supposed to be Caucasian, but instead was black and blue and purple and yellow, with scraped areas on his left cheek scabbed over the color of oak bark. The hiss and click of the ventilator breathing for him maintained a monotonous rhythm in the chilly room.

"So anyway, that's Don," Thalia said, gesturing toward him. Her mask of makeup was back in place this morning. She wore dark jeans and the black toeless booties, with a low-cut lavender pullover stretched tightly across her bust and the roll of extra weight at her midsection.

"Nobody here can tell me one way or the other what to expect. So he's just running up another goddam bill, the way he does," she said, shaking her head in frustration. "Even with his insurance this is going to be crazy expensive."

"Tell me about his fall, and then I'd like to know about the affair he's been having. And then maybe you could talk about your financial situation. Whatever you're willing to share."

"Let's go down to the cafeteria. They say even if he's in a coma he can still hear us. And I can get some coffee and warm up a little."

The image of the Hierophant card reversed, the card at the center of Thalia's reading, came to mind: the man who isn't listening.

"Besides," Thalia said, "what I'm gonna tell you might give him a heart attack, which just means the cops can accuse me of trying to murder him twice."

We took the elevator down and I bought coffee for her and iced tea for me.

"So he's a dick, okay?"

"I got that part," I said. "How long have you been married?"

"Twenty-four years. We were fine, or so I thought, until last year, when our youngest moved to Denver and the house was empty. That's when the fuckwit behavior started."

She put her lips to her coffee, made a face, and reached for two packets of sweetener.

"This stuff is pure cancer, but sugar is poison

too," she said, shaking the packets at the top edge before ripping them open and upending them into her coffee. I took a sip of my unsweetened tea.

"What was Don like when you met?"

"Kind of a country boy, very sweet and unsophisticated and loving. I fell hard for him after dating a lot of know-it-all city boys. He grew up around horses and whenever we visited his home he went back to sounding like a hayseed. But then Don moved into technology and got promoted to a management job at Chevron, so he made an effort to talk like everybody else.

"His mother raised Arabs, good ones. And even though we live on an eighth of an acre in Piedmont Pines and she lives in Missouri on a zillion miles of pastureland, she gave him a dapple gray Arab filly a few years ago. So we needed to stable and feed and shoe and saddle her, and then buy an RV/trailer and a gas-guzzler truck with a tow hitch — oh, and then pay the vet whenever the horse hiccupped. Thousands every month. What a 'gift.' And since then he's bought two more horses because he caught the long-distance race bug and he says he has to have at least one horse ready to go every weekend."

She rolled her eyes.

"He has a big salary, which meant I could quit my old job, but I pay all the bills, so I know exactly how much the horses cost. I wound up paying for a lot of the upkeep out of my own savings, even though I don't ride. I tried to learn, but Don told me I had no aptitude and basically kicked me off the horses and canceled my lessons. Now I think it was just his way of keeping me out of that part of his life so he could try to score with the younger women at the barn. Anyway, if I hadn't contributed money from my inheritance and my 401(k) we'd be neck-deep in debt. As it is, there are things we postponed because, for Chrissake, the cash was all going to the damn horses. So I took the clerical job at Yolanda's firm to bring in some more income."

"Tell me about the Tevis Cup, and how he fell."

"How much do you know about the Tevis?"

"Assume I don't know anything."

She held her coffee cup to her mouth and blew on it. She put it down again and stirred it with a wooden stick. Still undrinkably hot; still carcinogenic.

"Okay, so the Tevis Cup is a twenty-four-hour ride every year up near Lake Tahoe," she said. "Actually it starts closer to Truckee than Tahoe, and it finishes near Auburn, heading southwest through this wild, mountainous terrain. It's supposed to be the route settlers took through the Sierras. Or whatever. I think some crazy guy decided to do the first one-hundred-mile ride in one day on a dare, and after he succeeded the ride became an annual thing."

"I hear it's a big deal."

"Among trail races it's a very big deal. Riders come from all over the world — Saudi sheiks, that kind of thing. It's sort of like a road rally, and there's all these checkpoints and maximum times you can take between the checkpoints, and vets are checking your horse all the time, making sure it's sound, pulling you out if the horse is in trouble. The race starts on a full-moon weekend so the riders can see where they're going after dark, because everything kicks off Saturday morning at dawn and finishes Sunday morning at dawn."

"It sounds like a lot of preparation and effort go into it."

"No shit. Anyway, I'm Don's crew, not that I ever applied for the job. It's all dust and heavy lifting and horse shit and truck exhaust, all that effort just so you can get a really bad sunburn, is what I think. But anyway, Don and I drove up together, hauling the RV trailer with our food and Buddy and Peaches and their food. Don was set to ride Buddy, our big Arab gelding, and Kyle, Jenny's son, was entered on Peaches. Peaches is our original Arab, and she's smaller than Buddy but very strong and she has terrific stamina. Jenny the whore homewrecker has her own horse. They were all going to ride together so Kyle could learn. I had to stand there and watch them saddling up, making goo-goo eyes. Kyle knows they're screwing and so do all the other young riders. He blabbed it after one of the girls who helps tend the horses asked Kyle a question about Buddy's feed and Kyle walked into the RV where they were going at it."

She shook her head and made a "puh" sound of disgust.

"Classy," I said. "And that must have been awful for Kyle."

"After that little episode the barn manager kicked Don's RV off the property, so now we have the damn thing sitting in our driveway blocking the garage. Don said he was going to find someplace to store it, and I know he wanted to because that's where he and Jenny can get together, but so far it's just an eyesore for the neighbors to complain about."

We were quiet for a moment, sipping our respective caffeine and cancer crystals.

"Where did Don fall?"

"Not too far from the start there's this section of the trail called Cougar Rock. The trail narrows and falls away on either side of this steep climb and then drop-off. Buddy slipped and Don went down under the horse. Somehow his helmet came loose so he smacked his head and his arm and leg were smashed. Buddy got right back up again, but Don was a mess."

"Why aren't the police calling it an accident?"

"There were other riders around. And there's this volunteer team of riders with HAM radios that called in the accident and they got Don med-evacked out. My impression is that somebody said something to the race people and they re-layed it to the police, and the police came after me. But I don't know for sure. I haven't heard an-ything from them for the last few days."

"Why is he back here instead of up in Truck-ee?"

"Because I had him transferred down here once he was stable enough. He got medical treat-ment pretty quickly, considering the terrain is so remote. The race organizers are prepared for emergencies with riders or horses or both."

"Why a San Francisco hospital instead of one in the East Bay closer to you?"

Given the Bay Area's horrendous traffic, a hospital requiring a two-hour round trip to visit on any regular basis was an adversity that would be difficult to describe as "sweet."

"Because the Tevis people told me the best neurosurgeons and orthopedic people were here. And also to keep Jenny away if I could, because it would be 'inconvenient' for her to drop in, not that it's stopped her. She sashays around every-where with the biggest sense of entitlement you've ever seen. 'Whatever Lola wants,' that kind of attitude."

Thalia tried her coffee again and took a swal-low. When she looked up at me her glance went to the cafeteria doorway. She put her cup down abruptly, coffee sloshing onto the laminate table top.

"Oh for Chrissake. Shit shit shit," she spat, clenching her fists and jumping upright, her chair scraping the linoleum floor.

I turned around to look. Blonde with high-lights, possible breast implants, lots of jangling silver bangles.

Given Thalia's bloom of rage, verbal confir-mation of the whore homewrecker identity seemed unnecessary. The Seven of Wands image, with those people battling each other, flashed in front of me. If someone was going to keep chair legs from flying around the room doing substan-tial human damage, it was going to have to be me.

≈**11**≈

"Listen to me, please please just listen to me for one second," Jenny said as Thalia and I walked toward her. Well, I was walking; Thalia was stalking, stiff-legged, stiff-armed, bent forward at the waist. If she'd been an elephant she'd have been trumpeting, rocking back and forth and hurling dust around with her trunk.

"You have no right to be here. I'm going to call security and get your cheating whore ass thrown out of here," Thalia said, jabbing her finger at Jenny. From the other tables in the cafeteria heads turned to see what was going on. One woman in a white lab coat pulled out a cell phone and punched her finger on the screen. She was calling security or filming the next viral YouTube video, I couldn't tell which.

In spite of Thalia's rage, I've learned that

when someone asks you to listen to them, unless they're at that sloppy drunk stage where a "how-NASA-staged-the-moon-landing" theory is about to be unleashed, it's a sensible idea to give them a couple of seconds. That old Hierophant card again.

I stepped in front of Thalia, my back to Jenny. I held up my hands, palms out and patting the air to stop Thalia's lavender talons from their forward progress directly toward Jenny's eyeballs.

"Thalia? Could you give us a minute please? Not for very long. After that I'll make sure she goes."

Thalia glared at me, perhaps a flicker of suspicion that I was betraying her just like her husband had done, but I nodded my head and smiled at her with the "I've got this" look.

"Don't let her into his goddam room," she said. "I had to raise holy hell to keep her out of there, and I don't want her sneaking back."

She was jabbing her finger over my shoulder at Jenny.

"Absolutely not. I promise you," I said, still patting the air between us.

"Like you're the only one who cares about him," Jenny said, leaning to her right to square off against Thalia from behind the barrier of my shoulder.

I turned around. "You shut up, right now, unless you want both of us to kick your ass and put you mostly dead into one of the rooms upstairs," I said.

Yep, that's me, the conflict de-escalator, picking up my own Wand and swinging it around in the middle of the fray.

I am not an inconsequential woman. I stand five-foot-nine and weigh somewhere around one-thirty-five, and Thorne has schooled me in multiple martial arts. Jenny looked to be about five-two and an even hundred pounds. She looked back and forth from my height to Thalia's heft and made a "hmmmph" sound. With it came the smell of too much tuberose-scented perfume, or maybe it was an unfortunate blend of stock, gardenia and lily.

I turned back to Thalia.

"Please. Just sit with your coffee for a couple of minutes and let me find out what she's going to say. If it's nothing, I'll cut the conversation short and escort her out of the hospital."

"You will do no such thing," Jenny said. "I can be here if I feel like it. It's a free country."

I turned around to her again.

"I will do absolutely whatever the hell I want to do with you. Is that clear? You don't seem to get it that right now you would be sporting a black eye and a concussion if I weren't stopping her. I'm willing to listen to you, which Mrs. Thalassos most certainly is not. If you actually have something worthwhile to say you will do exactly what I tell you to do, and be courteous and prompt while you do it."

I love how women talk to each other when they're pissed off. One of my wounded-bird ex-boyfriends was flabbergasted by my description of a work disagreement with a female colleague, a disagreement peppered with "I feel thisses" and "Well I feel thats." He told me that a man in my situation would just say, "Fuck you," and walk away.

So I considered a "Fuck you" in this situation, but there was the Hierophant, that rascal with his long earflaps, reminding me that this whole experience was about listening, about the connection we make with others, and about the disconnect that occurs when we shut down our willingness to listen to others and to our own inner voice.

As much as I wanted to swat Jenny flat-handed and watch her go splat on the polished floor, I held back.

"Jenny and I are going to the lobby," I told Thalia. "I won't be long."

I held out my arms, one behind Jenny's back and one aimed at the lobby down the hall, to get her moving toward the seating area near the hospital entrance.

Thalia stood where she was, watching us go.

⟨12⟩

"Tell me what you want to say," I told Jenny.

We were standing in the lobby rather than sitting on one of the upholstered chairs by the window. Sitting implied a longer, politer conversation than I was planning to have. Visitors and staff walked past, in and out of the hissing automatic doors.

"Who are you? And why should I tell you anything?"

"My name is Xana Bard, not that it matters. Right now I'm the only one willing to listen to you. So talk, please, or else go away."

Jenny looked around, her aggrieved expression seeming to seek confirmation that she was being badly treated for no reason. Unfortunately for her, people in hospitals have their own grievances to cope with. She put her hand to her hair and thought better of it; her hairdo was caked with the sort of clay product people with fine straight hair use to give their style "texture." I think if she had actually stuck her fingers into it, the hairdo would have refused to let them loose.

"Something's not right upstairs," Jenny said, pointing upward.

"Specifics, please."

"I don't *have* any specifics," she whined. The specifics were being naughtily elusive, and she was blaming them for not being more readily apparent.

Getting information from Jenny was like trying to extract a splinter from under a fingernail.

"Then why do you think something is wrong? And who or what is it you're talking about when you say 'upstairs?'"

"With Don. Duh. And one of the nurses."

"Jenny, either you tell me something you've seen or heard that is evidence of 'something wrong,' or I'm walking you out to your car and making sure you drive away."

She sighed, her patience exhausted.

"Just listen, okay? I've been coming at night whenever I can because the wifey is here during the day and she makes such a stink about my coming."

"And?"

"I don't like the night crew. There's something off about the way they take care of Don."

"Off how?"

"Just off. I don't know exactly why. I got kicked out last night thanks to the wifey in there," she said, pointing to the cafeteria, "before I could pin down what's not right. Like last night a male nurse was definitely acting suspicious. I asked him for his name and he lied. And he had a needle thing in his pocket that fell out. What was that for?"

"Jenny, what medical background or training do you have?"

"I don't have to have any training to know that when somebody lies about his name and he's trying to hide a hypodermic or whatever, something is definitely not right."

"What was the nurse's name?"

"Bruce something. His last name ended in 'son.' But he told me his name was Jones."

She humphed and shrugged.

"Is that everything?"

"Isn't that enough? I'm telling you something is definitely wrong. It's bad enough that she knocked him off his horse. Now she's going to let him die."

She raised her arms and dropped them with a slap to her sides.

"What do you mean, 'she knocked him off his horse?'"

"Just what I said. She was there. She did something to make him fall."

"What did she do?"

"Everybody saw it. Don was over the rock and then she did something and he fell."

"Again, what did she do?"

"Ask *her*. She's the one who did it. I told the cops and they're going to get her for it."

I'd had enough.

"Well then, thank you for sharing your concerns. We'll check it out upstairs. Now it's time for you to go."

I thought she was going to say "You can't make me" and stick out her tongue, but she saw how I was looking at her and turned to the entrance.

I stood inside the doors watching her until she had crossed the parking lot, opened the driver's door of a red mini-SUV, and climbed in. When the car began to back out of its space I headed to the cafeteria.

≈13≈

"Would it be possible for you to either stick around until this evening when the night shift starts, or else go home for now and come back later?" I asked Thalia, who was standing arms-crossed and scowly-faced in the doorway to the cafeteria.

"I want to check something out tonight," I said, "but I'm not an authorized visitor."

"Why? What did the town bike tell you?"

"Something about a questionable nurse."

I elected to omit the accusation about Don's fall until we were someplace where Thalia's screaming would not disrupt the healing process of hundreds of patients.

Thalia made the "Puh" sound and waved a

hand to swat away the nurse information.

"It may be nonsense," I said. "But she took a risk approaching you, and I'm fond of giving people the benefit of the doubt when they do something difficult in an effort to be helpful."

"She's a lying cheating whore who loves to create drama is all she is. She's had affairs with half the men in Oakland and San Leandro and she's caused I don't know how many divorces. I don't trust her any farther than I could throw a truckful of Clydesdales."

"If you don't want to stick around tonight, or if you have to be home, why don't you let the hospital know I'm an authorized visitor? I'll check things out and let you know what I think when we talk tomorrow."

Thalia tilted her head and squinted at me.

"Yolanda told me you like to dig in and get involved with people's personal business, the messier the better. I think you're nuts, and I don't believe a word that homewrecker Jenny says, but okay, why not, for Chrissake. I'll talk to the nurses upstairs and let them know you're going to be around. I mean, by the time I get home I'd have to head straight back here to make the night shift, so forget that. As it is, I'm not going to be able to spend all my time here the way I've been doing. I have to get back to work. With Don not working I need the money from my job. After a week of sick leave he goes on disability, which is a big drop in his pay. And there's no way his insurance is going to cover all this."

"I'm sorry everything is so difficult for you, Thalia."

She shrugged and looked off toward the front entrance of the hospital. She looked back at me, her face lighting up.

"I have an idea," she said, without elaborating. "But I'll run upstairs first and let them know you're going to be here tonight."

"And maybe other times as well," I said.

Worried about her bright idea, I was going to pry, but she turned and waved goodbye, saying "Sure thing," over her shoulder, and was gone, slinging her hobo bag over her shoulder and marching toward the bank of elevators.

≈14≈

Well, it turns out the male nurse's name was Bryce, not Bruce, and he was off-duty for two days, so I made no progress in unveiling his rumored creepiness.

I sat in the very comfortable reclining chair next to the comatose man's bed, listening to the hushed voices in the corridor beyond the sliding curtain.

What on earth was I doing here? Why did I get myself into these situations so willingly? What could I possibly do to help?

No helpful ideas came to me. As the Magic Eight-Ball—every psychic's premier fortune-telling tool—would advise under such circumstances, "Ask Again Later."

I climbed out of the recliner and headed home.

≈15≈

The thick cream-colored envelope arrived the next day, full of reply cards and stamped return envelopes and engraved script.

DeDe Ironhouse and Bix Bonebreak, whose actual name turned out to be William Bickerson Bonebreak, were getting married in the Chapel of Grace at Grace Cathedral on Nob Hill. The chapel, much more intimate than the massive cathedral itself, was modeled after Sainte-Chapelle in Paris. The wedding reception was to follow at the Top of the Mark, a block away on California Street.

I was thrilled for them — as no doubt was everyone else except my mother.

"He's so *uncouth*," Mater lamented.

When Bix, a lantern-jawed boulder of a human who ran a metal fabrication business, heard that comment he'd roared his seismic laugh.

"Uncouth! I'm *lousy* with couth!"

Mater had broken up his youthful love affair with DeDe and was still resisting the reality of their reconnecting decades later after both were widowed. Not long before, I'd given Bix the big honking diamond he'd taken to Shreve and had made up into a custom-designed engagement ring for DeDe. I considered the donation of the diamond to be next-generation reparations.

I thought about Mater's version of meddling versus my own. In the spirit of "ask again later," I asked myself if I was out of line poking my nose into Thalia's adversity, and I listened for the inner voice that calls me "Child" to tell me the kindest possible truth.

"Help her," I heard, so okay. I stopped second-guessing my own meddlesomeness in this particular case. I only found out later that "help" is defined differently depending on what form the so-called help takes and who's on the receiving end of it.

I checked all the boxes on DeDe's deckle-edge reply card, indicating that I would be attending her wedding with my plus-one, even though in Thorne's case it was more like a plus-one-and-a-half.

≈16≈

"Okay, that's one problem solved," Thalia said when I spoke to her on the phone two mornings later.

"What problem is that?" I said.

"I sold the horses and that fuckmobile, Don's RV horse trailer. They're community property and my name is the primary borrower on the RV loan, so I put up a notice at the barn and boom! All sold for cash. I'd sell his truck if I could, now that he won't be needing it to haul the trailer anymore. But there's only his name on the pink slip, so no dice."

"I see."

This was the solution that had ignited such a happy expression on her face the other night. If Don did emerge from his coma, I could see the

Seven of Wands' free-for-all conflict becoming relevant again.

"It means I can pay the mortgage this month," she said, with a note of triumph in her voice, "and eat something besides ramen noodles for breakfast, lunch and dinner."

"Ah," I said, at a loss for a more eloquent comment. I like ramen noodles. Their preparation involves boiling water and pouring it over dry stuff in a cup, a process remarkably similar to making tea. At which, I think we can all agree, I excel.

"And how is he doing?" I said.

"No change. I go over there in the evening now, after the bridge traffic has died down a little, and sit there with a book. At least I'm getting some reading done. They have this comfortable chair in there and I wind up falling asleep. I wake up when they come in to take his blood pressure in the middle of the night and then I drive home."

"Have you noticed anything about the male nurse Jenny suspected of being weird?"

"Last night was the first time I saw the one I think she was referring to. He seemed okay to me."

"Any news from the police?"

"No, thank God. Not that I've heard lately, anyway. I think Jenny's the one who's blaming me, and since I wasn't there it's her word against mine. So what can the cops do?"

I didn't like the way she sounded when she said that. I told her I'd stop by that evening to keep her company in the hospital. I wanted to check out the nurse who had trouble remembering his name, and maybe ask Thalia a few more questions about what happened at Cougar Rock. It nagged at me that the Widowmaker card, the Queen of Swords, had led off Thalia's reading.

≈17≈

As soon as I hung up from Thalia the landline rang again. If it had been my cell phone I'd have heard the melody of "She Drives Me Crazy," Mater's unique ringtone, but the landline just chirped without an editorial comment and "L Bard" was displayed on the handset screen. I couldn't tell if it was Mater Louisa or my sister Lulu, so I picked up and said hello, and here came some more not-so-sweet adversity.

"I'm coming up next weekend for the Best Ball tournament at the Club," Mater announced, minus preamble niceties such as "Hi honey," and "How are you?"

Mater employs a straight-to-the-bullseye approach to conversations with her offspring.

Since she was coming up to San Francisco for

the tournament, the Club she meant was the Olympic Club, where she and all her society pals are members. In Pebble Beach, where Mater lives, she is a member of the Monterey Peninsula Country Club, where she plays at least twice a week, rain or shine, and holds a ten handicap. When she triumphs in tournaments by shooting mostly even par there is muttering that she sandbags during regular rounds in order to retain her high handicap's unfair advantage. Probably true.

You don't want to get between my mother and the tournament champ's Waterford vase, pronounced "vahz."

"The golf sounds like fun. Where will you be staying?" I asked.

I no longer reflexively offer Mater a place to stay. Not that I don't have a comfortable guest room with en suite bath available for her; it's that she flirts shamelessly with Thorne and it pisses me off. He's invariably aloof and courtly in his treatment of her, so I don't know why I lose my cool. Nevertheless lose it I do.

Louisa Duncan Livingston Monaghan Bard, originally of Darien, Connecticut, is currently between wealthy husbands and seems convinced that plausible hair color and expensive cosmetology have preserved her grimly nurtured youthfulness and sex appeal. She refuses to be discouraged by male courtliness and aloofitude.

Anyway, my sister Nora lives five minutes

away in a mansion with plenty of room for Mater, so by shirking a hospitality offer I'm not exactly asking my mother to pitch a tent in a homeless encampment.

"I'll stay in one of the Club's downtown guest rooms so that I won't be any trouble to anyone," Mater said. "I'll drive up and meet DeDe and Charlotte at the golf course the next morning. We're playing the Lake Course, which is so much nicer. That wind on the Ocean Course is just dreadful."

"It sounds like a great time for you all."

"It would be fun for you as well, if you'd like to play. Ann has had to drop out of our foursome and we're allowed to have a non-member join us, if that player is family."

Mater has done everything in her power to lure me to the links. She's given me golf clubs and bag, a battery-powered club caddy for walking cart-free courses, shoes, gloves, windbreaker, tees, visor, enameled ball markers, club covers, a giant umbrella, distance calculator, lessons, stubby pencils, the works. Mostly the like-new equipment sits in the garage gathering dust.

The fact that Mater was inviting me to play golf meant she had exhausted her other options for rounding out the foursome. I am fond of DeDe Ironhouse and Charlotte Swansdon; they're a lot of laughs, which would be a plus with Mater focused entirely on the Waterford rather than the long cheerful sun-drenched walk watching birds and deer and trees that is what I believe the game of golf should be.

Anyway I said I would go.

"Promise me you'll take a lesson before Saturday," Mater said. "We have to use at least two of your drives and last time the only reason we could use your second one is because it bounced off a tree back onto the fairway."

She was right, so I promised.

≈18≈

That night at the hospital I sat next to Thalia, both of us reading while Don remained steadfastly comatose. I was in the middle of Sue Grafton's *X* and Thalia was reading *People* magazine.

A little after midnight two people drew aside the privacy curtain inside the door and came in: a medium-height brown-haired Caucasian man in blue scrubs with a stethoscope slung around his neck and a tiny woman I guessed was Filipina wearing a flowered smock and blue scrub pants.

The woman used a paper towel to erase the names on the whiteboard listing the day shift's attending staff and with a green whiteboard marker wrote "Bryce" next to the RN space and "Elissa" in the CNA space.

"Okay if we take care of him now?" the man

asked Thalia. I studied the nurse to see what I could discern from his tone and facial expression, as well as from that inner sense we all have about whether someone is a good soul or a jerk. I picked up a tinge of jerk, but I have no clear idea why. Some whiff of self-regard, superiority, dissembling, watchfulness? Maybe.

Thalia and I stood up to get out of their way as Bryce and Elissa proceeded to take Don's blood pressure, shift him around to adjust his bedding, check his foley bag, fiddle with the IV stand. They finished up with taking his vitals and pulled the curtain closed again as they left the room. They were quiet and careful and efficient as they went about activities that they must have done dozens of times a day for every day they were at work.

"Your thoughts?" I said when they were gone.

"I wish Don would die," Thalia said, and in the dim light I watched her cheeks bloom pink and her eyes brim over.

"Oh for Chrissake," she said, and got up to grab a tissue from the box on the side table.

"I meant about the nurse," I said, when she had recovered herself and was sitting again.

"No idea. Not a big focus of my attention right now. Because if that nurse is planning to do something awful to Don, I'm not sure I mind."

"Except the police may decide you were responsible. You said they already suspect you, and you're here every night, after all."

Thalia stared at me, her eyes wide.

"Oh for Chrissake. That's it then. I'm going home and staying home."

She looked around her chair for her hobo bag and shoved her magazine into it.

"Jenny can have him if she wants. I'm not going to give anybody any extra chances to accuse me of trying to hurt, much less kill, my fuckwit husband."

She yanked her coat on as she headed for the door. I watched her sweep the curtain out of her way as she marched out. In her wake the fabric swung back into place.

I sat listening to Don's slow breathing. I smelled floor polish and rubbing alcohol and fading patchouli, until I realized I had no idea what to do next, except go home. So I went home.

≈19≈

At last those women were gone, Bryce thought. The wife and that other one, the tall blonde who had looked at him in that assessing way. He and Elissa had done everything by the book with those two watching, but now they weren't watching.

Dilaudid this time. It was important to mix up the way you handled each situation so there was no pattern except for the result.

Narcotics were so easy. They came in standard sizes but the prescribed dose was very often less than the amount in the manufacturer's packaging. So the Pyxis machine automatically dispensed the prescribed dose and the RN was responsible for tossing into a sharps bin the unused remnant of the drug.

There was supposed to be a witness when you disposed of any leftover narcotic, but when it was busy you could excuse the support staff and then it was easy to slip the remainder in a pocket. It happened all the time, no big deal.

Bryce had been stockpiling leftover Dilaudid from the amputee patient in room 415 for the last three days. He'd checked the computer and this ICH patient had a Do Not Resuscitate order, plus an organ donor permission, so everything was all set. The syringe was in his pocket, and tonight was the night Mr. Thalassos was going to start donating organs.

So easy. Disconnect the IV, insert the syringe in the IV port on this guy's left hand, press the plunger, reconnect the IV so the saline bag would flush the drug from the port, walk away quickly and then run back when the alarm sounded.

The charge nurse would call the wife, and the reality was that many more people died in the wee hours compared to the daytime, so Bryce was confident he had completed another commendable effort. The world was going to be better off without Mr. Thalassos. He would die so others could live.

Bryce poked into his ear with the nail of his pinky finger, just in case there was wax accumulating. He'd read that if your ear wax dried rather than staying damp it meant you were unlikely to sweat and have bad body odor. Whether or not that was actually true, Bryce rarely broke a sweat after delivering a patient from misery and pain.

≈20≈

Thorne had waited up for me. He opened the door of his garage-level apartment and watched as I pulled the Chrysler in and turned off the ignition.

"Yes," I said when he opened the car door for me and took my hand to help me stand up. I meant "Yes, please let me keep company with you."

"They've been out," he said, as we heard the dogs' claws scrabbling on the kitchen floor above us. I knew Thorne had done what needed to be done with the pets, because what needs to be done is what Thorne always does.

Now, as he led me into his candlelit bedroom with the backyard Japanese garden shadowy and moonlit beyond the picture window, what needed to be done was that he brushed my hair and undressed me while Julian Bream strummed his guitar through the speakers.

When he began to rub my feet I knew this was going to be a good one. But then, with Thorne always doing what needs to be done, they are all without exception good ones.

ך   ך   ך

"What?" Thorne said, when we were quiet again in his bed, after he had swabbed the sweat from me with a warm washcloth and dried me with a heated towel. He tucked the duvet around my back as we lay skin to skin.

"I have no idea what I'm doing," I said.

"About?"

"Thalia in particular, but also in general. Why am I so eager to be drawn into situations like hers? Why am I such a happy warrior when someone is suffering but it's none of my business? Why don't I just sympathize and walk away like anybody with common sense would do?"

Thorne didn't venture an observation. He knew I was hashing this out for myself by talking it through the way women do, no male-proffered solutions required. He was just listening, which is a stellar way of connecting with and endorsing the judgment of the one you love.

"In Thalia's case my response was almost automatic. I didn't hesitate. I think maybe that's what has me alarmed. I know we all have behavior patterns we fall into unless we're careful and thoughtful, and maybe that's what I've fallen prey to in her case. Because really, what can I do for her? Her husband is going to live or die without any help from me. She's going to stay married or get divorced or widowed without any help from me. The police are going to arrest her or not without any help from me. And Mater is going to win the golf tournament this weekend or not, I guarantee without any help from me."

I told him about my mother's invitation to play at the Olympic Club.

"Eugene is a pro," he said.

Thorne has friends who do pretty much everything on earth.

"Yes, please. Anytime this week."

So my golf lesson was arranged for.

"But the other stuff I was talking about. I feel like my wounded-bird rescue impulse is still going strong, just not with boyfriends anymore, thank God."

I kissed Thorne's shoulder. We were quiet.

"A suggestion?" he said, his heavy head above mine, his soft mouth at my ear.

"Please," I said, having hashed out as much as I felt I could manage on my own. I don't mind suggestions as long as the suggester asks permission to lay one on me. It's the unsolicited ones that irritate.

"You're good at it," Thorne said. "Maybe that's why it feels right to you. Maybe your angels guide you."

"Because every single time I manage to find the lighted pathway through the dark scary forest."

He nodded, his mop of blond hair brushing my forehead.

"I need to feel more connected to that then," I said. "I need to ask my inner voice to weigh in before I go barging heedlessly into something. That voice that calls me 'Child' never leads me astray. Always to the lighted path."

He nodded again.

"Good talk," I said, kissing his neck.

I turned so that we could spoon as the moonlight reflected off the ocean shining through the window.

The candles guttered in their dishes and went out while we slept.

≈21≈

Something else had happened while Thorne and I slept; Don had died.

"They called me right away when his monitors started beeping," Thalia said when she phoned in the morning. "Apparently the swelling in his brain was just too much. His driver's license showed him as an organ donor, and I told them to go ahead and take everything that would help someone else in the world. So anyway that's it for Don."

"I'm very sorry, Thalia. This has all been really difficult for you."

"No shit."

She was silent. I waited for her to ask before offering to be helpful. I didn't bother my inner voice about what to do. Sometimes just allowing the other person instead of your better angels to guide you is the right move.

"Xana, would you mind if I asked you to do something a little crazy?"

Thalia had used my name for the first time, and she was asking for help politely.

"I'm pretty sure I won't mind, but you should probably define crazy for me first."

"I want to go back up to Truckee, to where the accident happened, and try to revisit everything. I would really like you to go with me. Actually to drive me, if you can. My car isn't as reliable as it used to be and Don's truck is joined at the hip to the gas pump. And also could you please come to the funeral? I'm worried that Jenny is going to show up, because I wouldn't put anything past her, and I know I'll start slapping her around unless I have a hall monitor holding me back."

"When is the funeral?"

"Tuesday evening at Demetriou's Mortuary in San Leandro is the viewing. The funeral is Wednesday morning at the Greek Orthodox church. But first I'd like to go up north tomorrow, if that's possible." She paused. "I know what I'm asking is crazy."

"Give me a second to think about it," I said.

I asked my inner voice what to do.

I heard "Go."

"I'm in," I said. "With a condition."

"What?"

"No patchouli oil please. It's a long drive in a confined space."

"You're kidding."

"Not kidding."

She took a few seconds. I imagined blossoming resentment followed by a curt cancellation of the junket.

"Deal," she said, and sighed.

I felt very brave to have broached a personal hygiene topic with her, and relieved that my car's leather seats weren't going to reek of the neo-hippy passenger for an unspecified but way-too-long period after our trip.

Much later I realized I should have asked Thalia, not my inner voice, some more questions. Lots more.

≈22≈

My niece Jun-Ma, one of my sister Nora's many adopted kids, characterized the mighty Hemi engine in my Chrysler 300 as "a safety feature." The Hemi instantly goes *vroom vroom* when necessary. I seem to find vrooming to be necessary pretty often.

Because cruising America's splendid interstate highway system smoothly, quietly, at eighty-five miles per hour, past drivers for whom the posted speed limit apparently exerts an undue influence, is perfectly safe in that tight, quiet, comfortable sedan. I am confident this is true, whether or not the California Highway Patrol agrees with me.

Seriously: what part of "fast lane" is so difficult for other drivers to grasp?

I picked Thalia up in the Oakland hills. Her aging Subaru Outback was parked in the driveway, its sun-bleached roof paint corroding from tan to a blotchy silvery cream color.

She came out of the house through the garage and walked past the horse trailer RV, and while the garage door was open I saw that this was one of those garages that is too full of stuff to perform its essential job, which is to keep your precious vehicle safely indoors, free of bird droppings, sun bleaching, dripping pine sap, meteorites, all that impending damage.

I glimpsed horse tack, mountain bikes, snow ski equipment, a jet ski, rolling coolers, an ATV, tennis and racquet ball racquets, and enormous blue Rubbermaid bins with lids. I guessed camping equipment was in the bins but they could have been storing anything, including nuclear fission components.

We were both wearing T-shirts and jeans, she layering hers with a plum-colored zip-front hoodie and me sporting a baby blue cotton cardigan. She threw a jean jacket in the back seat; I had put my navy blue suede jacket in the trunk before driving across the Bay.

I decided to drive "against" the "flow" of morning traffic, even though the morning, midday and evening traffic in the Bay Area is vile in every direction, and we headed down the hill to Highway 13, then south to 580 toward Dublin, before shifting north on 680 to Fairfield. From there we merged onto Interstate 80 east.

We didn't talk much as we headed steadily uphill into the Sierras. Thalia may still have been simmering over the patchouli ban. I had the radio on quietly, playing the kind of inoffensive jazz that has replaced Percy Faith and Montovani in elevators these days.

Once we passed Truckee she started giving me curt directions. We exited onto state highway 267 south, and then at Brockway Summit she pointed out a narrow paved turnoff to the right, vaguely marked Watson Road.

From there it was a winding fourteen miles uphill and down at slower and slower speeds, skirting Watson Lake and turning northward to the Roble Equestrian Center alongside Forest Road Six. As we crawled along on the increasingly unpaved surfaces, I was glad I had opted for oversized 20-inch wheels, yet I still apologized to the car. We never scraped bottom, but the Chrysler was going to require a dust intervention upon returning home.

We pulled into a big dirt and gravel parking area, small boulders marking off boundaries, trees everywhere around us. I shut off the engine. With the air conditioning off, the car immediately began heating up in the bright sunlight.

"So how far is Cougar Rock," I asked, turning to Thalia. "I brought my hiking boots."

"Oh, you can't hike to Cougar Rock from here."

I stared at her.

"It's miles and miles down the trail," she said. "We'd have to take a helicopter, or ride a horse or a mountain bike or an ATV. But it would take a couple of hours to get there."

"I don't see our helicopter. Will it be here soon?"

"Ha ha, very funny," Thalia said.

I stared at her.

"I wanted you to see how wild this country is," she said, waving a hand to indicate our surroundings. "The Tevis route runs through total wilderness. It's really dangerous. There's this place called Pucker Point, because of what your ass does when you're riding along the edge of the ridge there, looking down into the ravine on your right. There's tons of places along the trail like that."

I stared at her. We had just driven four hours and were in the middle of the forest primeval with no lunch immediately at hand, no investigative purpose that I could see, no bathroom in sight, and another four hours ahead of us to drive home. I had brought my car mug full of iced tea, but the mug was nearly empty, as opposed to my bladder.

She shrugged.

"Were you there at Cougar Rock when Don fell?" I said.

"No," she said, shaking her head and looking

off into the trees outside her window.

"Jenny says you were."

Thalia turned and glared. She beat her fists on her thighs. "That bitch would. Well, she's lying. If you're not a rider or a Tevis Cup volunteer, you're not supposed to be on the trail. There are milestones where the support team can meet up with a rider. The vets check the horses out and riders can pee and get some food for themselves and their horses, medical attention, all that. But mostly the Tevis is the horse and the rider all alone trying to travel across a hundred miles of mountains and back country in twenty-four hours."

I picked up on a clue. All this way to no purpose, but wait, here was a clue.

"Was there a volunteer at Cougar Rock?" I said.

"I assume so. Sure. There always is. There must have been one to get Don out of there so fast after he fell. Riders back up at Cougar Rock waiting their turn, because their horses balk at going up and over. There's a side trail that goes around the rock that you can take and it's perfectly legal, but people who do this race are nuts. They think going over Cougar Rock is one of the biggest thrills of the ride. The No-Hands Bridge, Pucker Point, wading through the American River, all that stuff is insane if you ask me. But anyway there's videos on the website and on YouTube showing the route, and showing riders going up over the rock."

She was giving me a lot of information, but I felt like she was dodging the original question.

"How do we find the volunteer who was at Cougar Rock on race day?"

She turned to stare at me. "I suppose we call the Association that puts on the race every year. I dunno if they'll tell us who it was."

She shrugged and turned away.

"Have the police talked to him or her, do you know?"

"No idea. I'm not exactly seeking out conversations with cops since they started accusing me of causing Don's fall."

She paused.

"Wait a minute," she said. "If Jenny told the cops I was there, she's probably blaming me for his fall."

"Probably."

"I'll kill her."

"Um...Thalia?"

"Sorry. Sorry. But for Chrissake."

We were quiet for a few moments.

"So let me get this straight," I said. "We came all the way out here to the middle of nowhere, even though we wouldn't be able to see the location of the accident or talk to anyone who actually did see it?"

"Well, Jenny and her son Kyle saw it. They

were riding with him. And probably some other riders were there too, waiting for their turn to tackle the rock. Actually I don't think anybody really saw it, because it happened as he was coming down the far side."

"Why aren't Jenny and her son suspects, if they were the ones there with him? And why aren't we talking to them instead of sitting here in an empty parking lot?"

Thalia shrugged.

I opened my car door, first to let in the cooler air that smelled of sun-heated rock and fir trees, and also to let out some of my frustration. I swiveled to put my shoes on the ground and took one deep cleansing breath, and then another. I stood up and walked toward the nearest trees, feeling the sun warm my hair and shoulders, listening to an orchestra of birdsong. I looked up and there was a flash of black and white magpie wings flitting across the forest.

"Oh for Chrissake, don't be mad," Thalia called, standing outside the car, leaning her elbow on the roof.

I *was* mad, but the sun and the air and the trees and the birds had allowed me, and rightfully so, to blame myself rather than Thalia. I accepted that I had failed to clarify what this excursion was all about before I leaped to volunteer my time and my car. I had to face the unwelcome truth that once again I preferred being shot out of the starting gate instead of asking enough questions to determine if a given race was one I ought to run.

"Let's go," I said, climbing back in and pulling the car door shut. "I want lunch and a bathroom and Wi-Fi. We're going to watch some video of that damn rock. I have to say I'm a little annoyed, Thalia. We could have had lunch and a bathroom and videos without driving for eight hours round trip."

"Oh c'mon," she said. "I warned you it was crazy."

Well, she had.

Damn.

ר   ר   ר

We ate in Truckee, just sneaking into the Donner Lake Kitchen before they closed for the day at 2:00 p.m. I discovered that if you want them to, they will serve sliced avocado on anything you order, which I definitely wanted them to.

While we waited for our order, Thalia showed me video on her phone of riders queueing up to make their attempt at Cougar Rock, and sure enough there was a gray-haired white guy in a Day-Glo yellow vest standing just off the trail and reminding riders to keep their weight forward, or to feel free to take the trail around the rock to the right if they wished.

I watched one horse refuse and the rider reverse direction and return to the base of the rock. He made it over on the second attempt. I watched the next horse go straight up and over, and wondered how any sane person would want to put herself or her horse through that experience. But then people, me included, do some lunatic things and feel better about themselves afterward than they did before, so oh well.

This drive. I wondered if I would feel better about myself when it was over.

"Is the same volunteer there at Cougar Rock every year?" I asked.

"I don't know. Maybe."

"Do you know who to ask?"

"Not really."

I wondered about that. Her tone was off, somehow. I let it go and ate my avocado-laden lunch, asking the server to refill my iced tea car mug before we paid up.

On the way home we were quiet until, nearing Fairfield and the exit onto Highway 680 southward, Thalia said, "I've never lived alone."

"Ever?"

"Nope. I lived with my parents and then I lived with roommates and then I lived with Don."

"An adjustment, then."

"I don't know if I can do it. The kids are out on their own now. I thought I'd be glad about that, have a second honeymoon or something, but then Don started this goddam affair. These last few days in the empty house, I realize I don't want to live alone. I like being with a man."

"Me too," I said.

"You have a boyfriend?"

"I do."

"I didn't see any boyfriend stuff at your place."

"We have a living arrangement that works for us. It's not full-time."

She shook her head.

"I don't know what to do. I never thought I'd have to start dating again."

I took a chance.

"Well, the law seems to require all women who've been through a bad break-up to date John Mayer. Having sex with John Mayer appears to be a key step in the recovery process. A big plus is he'll probably write a song about you afterward."

Thank God she laughed.

"Except I'm not famous," she said. "He only dates famous women. With big boobs. But okay my boobs are big enough. That's one for my side."

She took the palms of her hands and shoved her breasts together. Impressive cleavage brimmed over the top of her T-shirt.

"There you go."

"Buy a bunch of push-up bras and keep the girls front and center. My body may not be the wonderland he's used to, but I'm motivated. Plus I like his songs."

"Sounds like a solid, achievable goal."

"Where does he live, do you know?"

"I think he bought a house in L.A. a little while back, after living in Montana for some years."

"You know some weird shit, Xana. But okay, I'll prepare for a pilgrimage to Los Angeles and Mr. Mayer. Because he's studly, although he is not a long-term solution."

"The transitional affair all the books say you have to indulge in in order to recover from a divorce."

I was careful not to call her a widow. I didn't think the term would sit well with her while she was imagining X-rated romps with John Mayer.

She giggled on and off all the way to her house in the Oakland hills, which told me I was right to shun the "W" word.

The traffic was vile.

≈23≈

When I dropped her off, I asked Thalia to let me use her bathroom, a critical path necessity after five hours of sipping iced tea in vile traffic. She fished around in her oversized purse and pulled out a garage door opener, which is what I was hoping for. I wanted to see what was in that garage because earlier something had triggered a semi-conscious urge to look more closely at things.

Thalia's was a pleasant three-bedroom two-bath house, with an overall beige decorating scheme and purple pillows and throws scattered around on the living room furniture. The kitchen we entered via the side door of the attached garage was all dark wood cabinets, black appliances, and deep black-brown speckled granite counter-tops. I found it gloomy, but it wasn't my kitchen, and Thalia had certainly succeeded if her goal was to minimize any evidence of dirt.

"Let yourself out of the garage when you're done, okay? I want to take a shower" Thalia said, pointing out the hallway bathroom to me and continuing down that hall to what I guessed was the master bedroom and bath.

No "Thank you for driving," or "Drive safe-ly," or any other chummy form of goodbye. Still resenting the patchouli ban, I feared.

"Sure," I said.

After the bathroom visit it suited me to be turned loose in the garage, and I took my time puttering around in there. There were two moun-tain bikes, one of them a woman's bike, purple and silver and black, with a battery assist. It was extremely dusty and there were pebbles in the tire treads. Okay, you ride mountain bikes in the dirt and they pick up dust and pebbles. But the other bike was clean. There was a green four-wheel ATV, also dusty and pebbly, with a Keep Tahoe Blue sticker on the front fender. If I were Holmes in London, I'd know within a five-yard radius where that ATV's dust came from.

I am not Holmes, or even Holmesian. I would need to ask Thalia about the bike and ATV. I thought it might be an even trickier conversation than the personal hygiene one.

I also wanted to find out who the volunteer at Cougar Rock was and ask him about Don's fall. I wanted to learn from Jenny exactly what she saw on race day. I wanted to talk to her son Kyle too, a particularly tricky thing to want.

But first, getting my priorities straight: a golf lesson.

≈24≈

I met up with Thorne's golf pro friend Eugene and dutifully kept my head down and back straight, adjusted my grip, watched video to see what Eugene meant when he coached me on moving my hips and wrists correctly, after which I hit a bucket of balls, with emphasis on my woods. We had to use two of my drives in a Best Ball tournament, and I was more capable using irons than woods, but woods are what you drive with on the longer holes.

I hate using woods.

On Saturday morning I was up at seven, dressed in lightweight glen plaid slacks, a white blouse with collar, and a black cotton sweater vest. My fleece-lined windbreaker, golf bag and shoes were in the trunk of the Chrysler as I drove down the Great Highway to Skyline Boulevard and the entrance to the Olympic Club.

I saw DeDe, wearing a black-on-black cashmere-blend sweater and a checked golf skirt, in the parking lot. She glowed the pink of peony buds and smiled with her well-kept teeth. We hugged hello and she flashed me her custom engagement ring with the big honking diamond. I made wowzah eyes at it and told her how I was looking forward to her wedding.

"How is the planning going?" I asked.

"Oh, that's all done. We're keeping it very simple."

"Very simple" for DeDe's crowd probably involved the Mormon Tabernacle Choir in Bollywood attire singing Handel's Messiah in Welsh as biscotti and VSOP brandy were passed around on gilt trays by reindeer-leading Laplanders, but we would see.

One of the Club's handsome male Pro Shop staff walked over to take my clubs and strap them onto a golf cart's rear shelf next to DeDe's bag. I sat on my Chrysler's open trunk lip and changed into my golf shoes. DeDe headed to the ladies' locker room to change into hers. I saw Mater's car coming down the Club driveway.

"Were you able to take a lesson?" Mater asked as she stepped out of her silver Lexus sedan. It wasn't the LS 500 with the turbo, so I pitied her.

She was wearing a fawn cashmere twin set and hounds-tooth slacks in fawn and black. Her chin-length believably light brown hair was held in place by a black velveteen head band, and gold coin earrings glinted.

"Yes I did," I answered. "And how are you Mother?"

She waved at the Pro Shop guy and when he saw her he pointed to her clubs, already sitting on the back of a golf cart next to DeDe's.

"From whom did you take the lesson?"

Mater generally ignores small talk and gravitates toward qualifying questions about other humans. If my golf lesson wasn't with Tiger Woods or Phil Mickelson, I was wasting my time and money. Worse, I was risking her Waterford vahz.

DeDe, bless her, showed up at that moment and asked Mater if her shoes were in her car or if a trip to the ladies' locker room was necessary, since our tee time was approaching.

Mater shot me an admonitory glance and turned toward the clubhouse locker room to change shoes. She keeps duplicate equipment at the MPCC and the Olympic Club so as not to have to transport bags and shoes and clothing back and forth.

I waved at glamorous blonde Charlotte, who appeared by the golf carts wearing a red cashmere turtleneck over a turquoise skort, and she waved back with scorecards in her hand. Charlotte's makeup was impeccable, as always, and her skin looked as close to a French porcelain doll's as a human's could, thanks to Botox and fillers. DeDe and I walked over to join her.

"I'm going to ride with your mother," Charlotte said, "because I'm a saint."

We laughed.

I would like to say I played well, but the Olympic Club Lake Course is not a forgiving experience for the casual duffer. It was made a little more playable by actual humans when a recent redesign took out quite a few trees. They also shortened the approaches on some holes, but even so the wind off the Pacific can blow your drive to Nebraska, and the greens are usually surrounded by voracious sand traps. The course is not flat by any means, so even with carts it's a lot of marching uphill to the greens, or chasing after your ball as it slides down-slope into the rough.

As one does, the four of us floated around a little on the golf carts, depending on where our lie was after our most recent stroke, so from time to time I rode with my mother. As we started the back nine I noticed she was standing up from the cart and immediately grabbing onto the windshield frame to steady herself.

At the fifteenth green I realized I'd never before seen my mother perspire, and her forehead was beaded up even though the fifteenth was a relatively level hole, the weather was cool, and there was a fresh breeze.

"Are you feeling all right?" I asked her.

"I'm fine. I think I must have eaten something that disagreed with me," she said, waving away my concern. I kept glancing at her over the next two holes, because something was wrong with her, even if she refused to admit it.

At the eighteenth tee, facing the famous IOU-shaped sand traps and the clubhouse beyond, Charlotte had the honors and stepped up to tee off. Mater, standing back and to the side with her three wood in her hand, began rubbing her jaw and her shoulder.

And then she fell down in an unconscious heap, her skin as gray-white as a burned-out lightbulb.

ᔆ25ᔆ

I volunteer with a third-grade class during the school year, which required me to learn CPR. I knelt next to my mother and felt her neck for a pulse, and then I leaned over her face to listen for breathing. Faint pulse, shallow breathing.

"Ambulance, right now," I called to Charlotte, and I continued to check my mother's pulse. "I think it's a heart attack."

Charlotte ran to her cart and careened down the cart path toward the clubhouse. DeDe went to her golf bag and pulled out her cell phone, a forbidden item on most golf courses.

"You never know," DeDe said as she pressed her fingertip to the phone to bring it to life, "but I turn off the sound and slip it into the bag. I never look at it or hear it ring while I'm playing, so it's no big deal."

I heard her talking to the main office at the club, and then to the 9-1-1 operator.

I don't know how long I knelt there on the grass, my fingers continuing to feel my mother's carotid and wrist. If the pulse had stopped, I'd have started CPR. If her breathing had stopped, I'd have started CPR. But she held on, tough old bird that she is. In case she could hear me, I decided to cheerlead in a way she would understand.

"Don't you dare leave us," I said, thinking of my two brothers and two sisters and zillions of nieces and nephews. "You hear me? You stay right here. It's not time for you to go. There are more Waterford vahzes out there and they are all of them, every single one, waiting for you and only you."

I was bossy with her because, as much as she drives me and pretty much everyone else insane, she is my mother and I can't imagine my world without her in it.

I lost track of time. I didn't feel the cold ground under my knees. I didn't hear the medical team arriving; I just knew they had pulled me upright and taken over. They asked me her name, and I told them what symptoms she'd been exhibiting.

The lead EMT began calling her "Louisa" in a loud voice and explaining what they were doing and that she would be okay. They hooked Mater up to IVs and lifted her onto a rolling stretcher, and then they trotted her to the ambulance parked on the cart path alongside the tee box.

"Do you know who her doctor is?" The EMT shoved the collapsing gurney into the truck.

"No, but he's in Pebble Beach, where she lives," I said. "Take her wherever you think the best cardiologist will be. She's got insurance up the wazoo."

"Do you have her insurance information?"

"Well, Medicare plus everything a person could possibly add to Medicare. It's got to be in her purse, in her car."

"We'll take her to St. Joseph's. Bring the insurance information."

"Yes. Fast as I can."

DeDe and I climbed into the golf cart and floored it back to the clubhouse. I told DeDe I would pick my golf bag up from her later, pulled Mater's car key from her golf bag on the back of Charlotte's cart, and opened the Lexus's trunk to grab Mater's purse. I jumped into the Chrysler after pulling off my golf shoes and drove in my stocking feet to St. Joseph's.

Knowing he would do what had to be done, I called Thorne en route and asked him to notify my two brothers and two sisters.

I prayed, because that's what you do. Pray hard, activate lead in foot, and make the Hemi engine go *vroom*.

≂2o≂

She was in a curtained "room" in the ER, vaguely conscious again, clad in a hospital johnny whose pattern of blue flowers on white cotton was worn blurry from laundering. An EKG's tentacles were stuck to her torso everywhere, the white wires climbing out the johnny's arm- and neck-holes. I stood back while the medical team rolled machinery in and out, injected stuff into the port on the back of Mater's hand, and handed me a bag with her clothes.

"Check that her jewelry is all there," a nurse said. I pulled out a cut-apart cashmere sweater set, cut-apart houndstooth slacks, an undamaged golf glove, golf anklets with fuzzballs at the back to keep them from sliding down at the heel, a black velvet headband, and golf saddle shoes with wet grass clippings stuck to them. A small bag held gold coin earrings, a heavy gold chain necklace, and the gold ring with topazes that Mater had been wearing at the golf game.

I expected everything in the hospital to smell of rubbing alcohol and Lysol, but instead there was the faint remnant of Mater's Shalimar perfume. Nothing defeats Shalimar.

A staff member in green cotton scrubs and a name tag that read "Keisha" approached with a clipboard and, after asking if I was the patient's daughter, took me to a cubicle to document Mater's insurance information and vital statistics.

Keisha was tall and slender and had deep umber skin, long maroon-polished fingernails and a pierced nostril. After entering Mater's information, she told me, "Your mother is stable, but it was definitely a heart attack, and we need to keep her for at least a few days for more tests and possibly surgery. Right now there isn't a bed in the coronary care unit, so we're going to get her upstairs and then move her when a bed in the CCU opens up. You can sit with her while we complete triage and get her admitted."

"Sure. Thanks."

So I sat waiting with my quiet but not unconscious mother. I was shaking, not from cold but from the shock of the experience. Someone noticed me shaking and draped a blanket around me. I clutched the edges together and said thank you. Except for the occasional nurse taking Mater's pulse and blood pressure, waiting was all we did.

I reached for my mother's hand. She felt mine take hers, looked at me, and I smiled. She gazed at me, pulled her hand loose, patted the back of mine, and clasped both her hands on her stomach.

Dr. Desai showed up sometime later and introduced herself. Petite, skin the color of almond husks, bright black eyes.

"She received ameliorative treatment very soon after the crisis, and we believe she will make a full recovery," the doctor said. "Surgery is still a possibility, along with changes to her diet and exercise routines. But with MIs it is critical to address the causative symptoms within minutes, if possible, so that there is no lasting damage. She was lucky to be with you and to have you call for assistance as quickly as you did."

MI: Myocardial infarction. Heart attack. Mater nearly died. It would take some getting used to, to accept that my tougher-than-Kevlar mother was actually mortal.

"I'm glad I was there," I said, and felt the adrenaline and the last of the shivers ebbing, finally, from my system.

"We are going to admit her, and keep her at least a couple of days, until we determine the best treatment options for her."

I nodded, and Dr. Desai left.

Time inched by, and then I walked alongside Mater as an orderly and an RN rolled her into the elevator and up to a room on the fourth floor that smelled of bubble-gum-scented room freshener. They lifted my mother onto the bed in the room, shifted her hook-ups to new machinery, tucked her in, asked if she was comfortable, and left.

Thorne walked in. I jumped up and threw myself at him, and he caught me and held on until I was ready to let go. We sat and he took my hand into his big roughened paw and waited with me, for what I had no idea.

"All except Brett," he said, meaning my California siblings would show up, but Brett lives in Chicago and wouldn't. I squeezed Thorne's hand.

Staff members brought in trays with liquids for Mater, which she ignored. She was either dozing on and off or had chosen to ignore the appallingly poor taste of her current situation.

Other staff members arrived frequently to take her blood pressure and check the readouts on a computer they hooked up to connections in the wall.

Thorne left for a few minutes and returned with turkey sandwiches from some machine, sandwiches that were dry without enough mayonnaise or tomato. We ate most of them anyway.

I called DeDe and gave her the update, speaking quietly because cell phones are supposed to be verboten in the hospital. DeDe promised to relay the word to Charlotte and Ann.

At eleven o'clock p.m. Bryce, the nurse who couldn't remember his name, walked in.

≈27≈

What the hell was this? Wasn't this the same woman who'd looked at him the other night in the organ donor's room, her stare so knowing, so judgmental? Here she was with the new MI patient, recognizing him, he was sure. Meanwhile, who was this guy who could play tight end for the Niners? And why was he looking from Bryce to the woman and back again?

Bryce felt his own gaze jumping around from the patient to the doorway to the two people sitting there holding hands. Ah, that's how the big man picked up that something was off; his girlfriend must have squeezed his hand.

Bryce lifted his pinky to his ear before catching himself. He put his arm back down to his side and forced himself to say hello and tell them he was going to take the patient's vital signs.

"The patient is Louisa Bard," the woman said. "I'm Xana Bard, her daughter. This is Thorne Ardall."

She nodded toward the Kong-sized man, but her eyes never left Bryce.

"You're Bryce, yes?"

He nodded that he was. So they were going to be watching him, were they? He felt something in his core start spinning. He lifted the clipboard at the foot of the bed, just to steady himself by focusing on something.

He wouldn't have much time, would he, with this patient only here for as long as it took to clear a bed in the coronary care unit. He knew from the shift briefing that the patient had had an MI, which meant she had disgusting eating and exercise habits — habits that were nearly impossible to get people to change, even if it meant a longer life. Probably a smoker, too; she was old enough to have started before the truth about tobacco was widely accepted. Maybe she was one of those fools who kept on smoking even though they knew they would die a painful death from it. In any case, it was only a matter of time before another more severe MI killed or incapacitated this woman, perhaps leaving her an expensive invalid for her family to care for, maybe for years.

And here came another of them, another sleek blonde woman who no doubt thought she could rule the world just because of her looks. This one was introduced as another daughter, Nora, and sure enough she resembled the tall blonde seated woman who jumped up to hug the newcomer. Nora then leaned over the patient to say hello, but no answer.

The big man bent to hug the new sister and stepped away so the women could sit and talk. He looked back to Bryce as soon as he had hugged Nora, and from where he was leaning against the wall he continued to watch Bryce taking the patient's vitals.

Then they all started talking about what to do. Bryce left the room while the two sisters blabbed. With a surge of rage Bryce flashed back to the third-grade recess playground, reliving the bullying he had received from Ryan and Josh, those two felons-in-the-making. They would knock him down, tear off his jacket on icy January days and throw it to each other, tell the teacher it was just a game, threaten to beat him up if he tattled.

He would not be bullied again, not by these three entitled blonds who thought they could stop him from doing what he did best. Bryce knew his purpose in life, and he was going to fulfill his purpose no matter how many glamorous speed bumps threatened to slow him down.

≈28≈

"I don't know what I should do," I whispered. Nora, with my blessing, had gone home to her husband and kids. I felt fretfulness, if not a full-on whine, in my voice.

Thorne turned to me, his light brown eyes with the green and yellow flecks glinting in the hospital bedside lamplight.

"Options?" he said.

"Stay here all the time and be her voice to the medical team. Ask my siblings to take shifts doing that job so I can have time off. Call Thalia and tell her I have a family emergency and can't help her anymore, or, option B, call Thalia and tell her I'll keep working on her situation but it will have to wait a couple of days until Mater's prognosis and treatment are clear. Another option, rapidly climbing the charts: go home, turn off the phones, climb into bed with all of my pets and swig mint tea while binge-watching 'Downton Abbey' and stuffing dark chocolate bonbons into my mouth."

Thorne smiled his infinitesimal smile.

"Ask," he said.

"Ask who? The sibs? Mater?"

Head tilted, he gave me the "you-know-what-I'm-talking-about" look.

I worked on remembering. He squeezed my hand, which I always enjoy.

"Oh yeah, the inner voice thingy."

He nodded.

"Okay, here goes."

I closed my eyes and asked myself what I should do.

"Child," I heard. "She's your mother."

I sent Thorne home to take care of the dogs and cats. I asked if he would please bring me non-machine-sourced food at some point, and he kissed my forehead as he stood up to go.

I pulled a pillow and blanket out of the room's closet, climbed into the reclining bedside chair, and tucked myself in.

Jenny had warned me about Bryce. On no evidence at all except my intuition, that old Hierophant card, I'd gotten a bad feeling about this nurse. Don Thalassos had died as soon as Thalia and I left him alone with Bryce. I didn't want to be the kind of daughter who left her mother alone with a possible angel of death. I'd figure out what the next steps should be after Bryce went off-shift in the morning.

≋29≋

I woke up from time to time when Bryce and another staff member pulled aside the curtain for check-ins on Mater's vital signs. I lay still in the chair and watched through half-shut eyes, and I saw nothing alarming.

There must be a gene for sleep, since I have no trouble fading out at a moment's notice, and I faded in and out all night until my sister Lulu arrived the next morning.

I shoved the blanket to one side, pulled my calves in to fold down the reclining chair's footrest, and hauled myself up and out to hug my sister. I bent over for the hug because Lulu takes after Mater instead of our tall father. Lulu is a gamine, petite and brown-haired, brown-eyed with a perennially mischievous smile lighting up her pale-peach complexion. She had on light-blue jeans, brown leather sandals, and a flower-patterned blouse tucked into her pants under a woven leather belt. Simultaneously pulled-together and Bohemian.

Thorne showed up right then, non-machine-sourced breakfast burritos in hand, and with Mater still ignoring all of us we settled down to review the situation and eat potato, egg, salsa, guacamole, and bacon-filled tortillas. Thorne pulled out his pocket knife and I cut mine in half for Lulu to share. I entered the exalted state to which such a burrito can elevate one, and sighed happily.

Mater awoke as we ate and in a querulous voice whimpered, "Lulu?"

"I'm here Mother." Lulu put down her burrito, stood up and reached for Mater's hand.

"*Finally* someone is here to take care of me," Mater said.

Lulu stole a look at me and I kept my face determinedly innocent of the nuclear eye-roll that was yearning to be launched.

Brett and Lulu, Mater's oldest and youngest, are always going to be her favorite offspring. Many expensive hours of therapy later I have learned to accept the sweetness of this adversity, in that I now know I am strong enough to be fully myself, and content about that, even without my mother's affection or approval.

"I've got this for now," Lulu said when Thorne gathered up the foil burrito wrappers and dropped them into the basket by the door. "I delivered a landscape to this guy who just bought a place on the 18th at Pebble, so I can take some time off."

Lulu is a fine artist whose works are popular with the Carmel and PB residents, including those show-offy plutocrats who can afford to buy a mansion on the fabled final fairway of Del Monte Lodge's Pebble Beach Golf Course.

"I'll be back tonight," I said.

"No need. Collin is driving up from L.A. He'll take the night shift. You've done the heavy lifting and you get a break."

"Brett?"

Thorne had said Brett wasn't coming, but Brett realizes he's Mater's favorite so you never know.

"On call, but for now he's staying in Chicago with the pork bellies."

"Ah."

Brett trades in pork futures from the City of The Broad Shoulders. He loves his pork futures something massive, along with deep-dish pizza, Buddy Guy, and a green river on March 17th. He loves them more than his mother, apparently, but who was I to judge?

I hadn't had enough sleep to avoid judging, is

what occurred to me. All my siblings had recently made the trip to San Francisco when my father was found murdered; therefore, begging off making a second trip so soon after that event was only sensible if Mater was already on the mend.

"Your plan?" I asked Thorne.

He twirled his index finger in a circle, indicating the current environment. I assumed Mater had either acquired bodyguard-able status, or that Thorne would spell Lulu when she needed a meal or a bathroom break.

"Thank you," I said.

I kissed Lulu's cheek, kissed Mater's forehead, kissed Thorne's lips in contravention of his general non-PDA policy, and waved goodbye. Time to go home and consider the options.

Whatever option I went with, I decided it would have to include dark chocolate bonbons.

≈30≈

The dogs were still twisting and moaning, demonstrating their elation at my return home, when my cell phone rang. I broke off petting them and cooing in the universal "good-doggy" voice all humans use, and pulled out the phone from my purse while leading Hawk and Kinsey toward the kitchen and the treat tin.

"Are you coming to the viewing tonight? Or the funeral tomorrow?" Thalia said as soon as I'd said hello.

"Remind me about where and what time?"

She told me, and I wrote the details down and said I would do my best to make it. It seemed pointless to mention my own family emergency, since Thalia's chromosomes appeared to be unequipped with the empathy gene.

Her call triggered my shelved curiosity about the way her husband had been injured. Setting aside the bonbon priority for the moment, I went online to the Tevis Cup website and there on the left of the home page was a list of photographers who work the race.

It took multiple calls to chase down the information about which photographers placed themselves at key locations along the trail to capture images that participants might want to buy.

The triumph of the telephonic pursuit was when I finally identified and talked to Hank Jessen, who had been at the crest of Cougar Rock. Jessen said he might have a shot of Don Thalassos and his fall.

"At least I should have one," Hank said. "But a lotta people come to grief at that damn rock, and those folks don't usually want a picture to make the memory of it permanent, if you know what I mean. So I sometimes delete those shots if nobody calls for one within a few days."

"Have you deleted all those shots yet?"

"I don't think so. But I take thousands a shots on race day, and there's always a crowd around Cougar Rock, so it could be tough to find what you're looking for."

"What kind of crowd? I thought the rock was pretty remote."

"Well, I'm not the only camera there. And there's volunteers taking shifts holding riders back 'til the previous horse makes it over or stops trying. So there's horses lined up waiting to make the attempt, and horses coming around the side of the rock on the flat trail, and people with walkie-talkies riding four-wheelers, waiting in case somebody's injured or going to call it quits, or sometimes the ATVs're ferrying volunteers and photographers like me back and forth to the next check-in point, that kinda thing. Cougar Rock is a busy place on race day."

"The man I'm looking for had a particularly bad fall. He had to be helicoptered out, is what I was told."

"Oh now I do remember that one. It's hard to miss a helicopter. And a lotta riders hadda be directed around the rock until that guy and his horse were taken off, and those other riders weren't too happy about missing the chance to go over instead of around. I think I took some shots of him, but not a lot. I figured nobody but the insurance people'd want photos, and so far nobody's called me about 'em. Plus I remember there were a couple a women yelling about the accident, and the volunteer medics had to keep 'em away. When the helicopter came I hadda put all my equipment back in the cases or the dust blowing around woulda damaged the lenses and gotten into the cameras."

He paused, realized how that sounded, and said, "I hope the guy's all right."

"I'm afraid he's not. He passed away a couple of days ago."

"Well, I am truly sorry to hear that."

I made an appointment to drive up to Sacramento and look through Hank Jessen's race-day files.

≷31≷

"Collin?" I asked Thorne when he walked into the kitchen after the dogs had calmed down. He nodded that Collin had arrived. My gay brother Collin lives in Santa Monica with his husband and they design CGI explosions for superhero movies. It's an endless source of income these days, and the lucrative work allows Collin to manage his own schedule. Thorne headed home after confirming that for today at least Lulu and Collin could trade off shifts watching out for Mater.

"Road trip?" I said to Thorne.

He lifted his inquiry eyebrow.

"To Sacramento. I tracked down a photographer who was at Cougar Rock. He offered to let me look at his contact sheets. You've got faster eyes than I do for that stuff."

Thorne has faster eyes than an osprey sighting a shimmering school of mullet in Narragansett Bay.

I went upstairs to the bedroom that acts as an office and rummaged around to find an old magnifying glass I could use for examining the tiny contact-sheet photos.

I heard Thorne open the refrigerator and begin pulling out food and drinks for the cooler, doing everything that needed to be done.

≈32≈

Hank Jessen was a sturdy man in a blue plaid flannel shirt and battered jeans, with a farmer's tan and a Kings ball cap on his graying, collar-length hair. He offered us liquid refreshment, which we declined, and then took us to a dining room table where there was a stack of pages with tiny images on them.

Thorne took one clump of contact sheets, I took another, and Hank took a third. I used my magnifying glass, but Thorne and Hank didn't seem to need one as they leafed quickly through the pages. It didn't take long for Thorne to find the photos of Don's horrible fall.

"These," he said, handing a page to Hank after quickly scanning the other sheets in his stack and ruling them out.

Hank took the page and held it up to the light. He took a pencil and bracketed a sequence of squares.

"Be right back," he said, and left. A few minutes later he returned with another sheaf of pages, each one with two enlarged photos printed top and bottom on the paper.

We saw Buddy, Don's big Arab gelding, rear and then topple when his back hoof slipped on the steeply sloped dust coming down the south side of Cougar Rock. The horse landed on his haunch and rolled sideways as Don's rein hands came up and the strap on his helmet unsnapped.

Riders are taught to kick their legs free of the stirrups if they know their horse is going to go down, and in that same split second they have to decide whether to hang onto the reins or let go. Don, as most experienced riders would do if out on the trail rather than in an arena, held onto the reins.

It's a long walk home if your horse bolts when you're in the middle of nowhere, and it's unsafe for the horse to be on the loose in the wilderness, not knowing the way home or how to escape predators or navigate trafficked roads.

But Don's foot caught in the stirrup, and there was a boulder between Buddy and Don's leg, and the same boulder caught the side of Don's helmet-less head and his rein-holding arm. Seeing the sequence of injuries in the photos was like watching the appalling fall in slow motion. I winced, seeing the visuals, and without meaning to my hand came up and covered my mouth at the horror of what I was looking at.

We flipped over the pages to see Buddy scramble upright and trot away downhill. Don lay motionless where he had fallen, a dust cloud floating down onto him.

≈33≈

We were quiet, the shocked silence that violence momentarily enforces. Then Thorne asked the right question.

"Why the buck?"

We went back to the contact sheets, scanning for photos of what preceded and succeeded the horse's rearing up.

"Those, yes?" I said, pointing.

Hank left again to print the photos.

"And how did Don's helmet come loose?" I said. "It looks like the strap just snapped open. That's not possible."

Hank returned with more photo pages. Before the fall, he had taken shots of a mounted woman and teenage boy coming over Cougar Rock. I recognized Jenny, and I figured the boy was her son, whose face was a cloud of fear and fury as his horse jarred him in the saddle descending the rocky path.

Thorne pointed at a photo, taken after Don's fall, of Buddy trotting away. There were people and boulders in the background of the photo. Thorne pointed, looking a question at Hank.

"One of the ATVers," Hank said, shrugging.

I took the magnifying glass to get more detail. There, mostly concealed by a boulder, was a fleshy dark-haired woman wearing a wide-brimmed straw hat and a purple knit top. I couldn't see enough detail in to be confident it was Thalia, but the ATV's wheels and dark green front fender with blue decal matched what I'd seen in her garage.

We looked quickly through photos of the heli-copter flying in and out with Don strapped down to a flat tray bed and loaded inside.

"Do you remember anything about the wom-en arguing? You mentioned that on the phone," I said.

"I just heard voices, really. I was mostly shielding my eyes from all the dust flying around. I think they were yelling about the horse and the accident. I think I heard the kid yelling too. But I really don't remember much except that I could hear their voices over the noise of the helicopter."

We scanned photos taken just prior to the fall. In one shot Jenny and her son Kyle waited side by side facing the trail they had just traversed. Kyle had his arm and fingers extended toward Cougar Rock, as if he were pointing. Or had just thrown something.

The woman on the ATV had something glittering in her outstretched hand.

⤳34⤳

Thorne drove us home after overpaying Hank for the pre- and post-fall photos, now folded into my purse. Overpaying for assistance of any and every kind is Thorne's primary religious practice.

Once again, as he so often did, Thorne asked the right question.

"Which one?"

"Hell if I know. Could have been either. Or both. Or neither."

"Why the son?"

"Maybe because he resents the affair? Thalia told me Kyle walked in on Don and Jenny one time up at the barn. If that's true, seeing your Mom having sex with someone not your father, or with anyone really, has got to be a pretty traumatic experience for a teenaged boy. And I don't know whether Jenny's husband knows about the affair and is about to divorce her. If that's true too, and Kyle opposes it, there's another motive."

"Thalia?"

"Well, she stands to lose all the way around in a divorce, which is what Don was demanding. She'd have had to give up her house, her smaller income would have left her in much poorer living circumstances, and I think she said her grown kids were upset about the divorce as well. But to murder him? I guess it's possible, but murder seems awfully harsh."

I thought about my conversations with Thalia.

"I think she lied, though. She told me she wasn't there. I definitely think that's her in the photo, on the ATV wearing purple the way she does. And what was that shiny thing she had in her hand?"

"A guess? Pellet gun."

My chin fell open.

"Oh shit," I said.

The phone rang.

"Hi Sis. They've moved her to the coronary care unit," Collin said. "I'm going to stay the night and Lulu is headed to your guest room."

"Thorne and I are on the way back from Sacramento. Ask Lulu if she knows where the key to the house is."

I heard Collin talking and Lulu answering.

"She knows where the key is," Collin said.

"How is Mater doing?"

"She's complaining about the incompetent staff, so I'm optimistic that she's on her way back to being her usual self."

"I'm glad she's leaving the fourth floor. There's a nurse there who strikes me as off, somehow."

"You and that pesky intuition of yours. You should ask Mater to let you read her palm so you could get the facts."

Collin is not sold on the idea that intuition can be trained and trusted, especially by the same cards with which we play War.

"The iffy nurse is a 'he'," I said. "I'm glad Mater is moved off his floor."

"Is he cute?" my gay brother said. "Probably. I think male nurses are always cute. Something about the helping professions. But anyway, with Mater complaining about the nursing staff you know it's because 'Thy Minions Shall Ever Fail To Live Up To Thy Standards.'"

Collin is the official repository of the White Anglo-Saxon Protestant commandments. "Thy Dog Shall Be A Labrador Retriever," that sort of thing.

"Thanks for coming all this way and keeping watch. I love you Sweetie," I said.

"You too, Pumpkin."

We hung up, and I looked up at Thorne.

"Pellet gun," I said.

He nodded. I remembered in Thalia's reading the prominence of the Queen of Swords, the self-created widow, and wondered how I would manage to broach to Thalia the evidence of Hank Jessen's photographs.

≈35≈

Bryce pulled his pinky finger out of his ear and examined what he had pried loose with his long fingernail. The magazine article that hypothesized that people whose earwax dried solid were unlikely to need much in the way of antiperspirants came to mind. Because as he watched the bitchy MI case being wheeled away to the CCU where a bed had finally opened up, to his surprise he felt his armpits prickle.

She was getting away, and those entitled blond offspring keeping watch over her had defeated him, and there was nothing he could do about it.

For now.

≈36≈

The funeral crowd was meager, but the service took place on a weekday morning, so perhaps Don's Chevron friends couldn't get away from work. Thorne and I, he in a charcoal suit, gray dress shirt, and solid-color olive tie and I in a navy dress and black flats, sat in a rear pew of the Greek Orthodox Church. We stood when everyone stood, sang the unfamiliar hymns, and listened to the psalm readings and the eulogy. We scooped a spoonful of koliva cake into a little bag when everyone else did. After we all sang "May Your Memory Be Eternal" the service wrapped up.

We didn't approach the open casket and we

didn't go to the burial, which turned out to be just as well, since there wasn't a burial. Instead, we shook hands with people as we walked out and drove back across the San Francisco Bay to our favorite café, the East-West in Daly City, where we were vastly overdressed for the early afternoon ambience.

We checked on the always hilarious specials Rose Sason had chalked on the blackboard. Her Philippine-inspired cuisine collaborations with Manny the Guadalajaran chef had resulted today in "Fish Lumpia Tacos with Chip Hotly Guac."

Thorne is, as one would expect, more intrepid than I am when faced with Chip Hotly, and he ordered the special and managed to ingest it without festooning his nice suit with guacamole. I ordered a "Scissor Salad" with grilled chicken and was intrepid enough to have the white anchovies.

"The conundrum," I said, as we sat afterward sipping our refilled drinks.

Thorne leaned back against the booth and gave me his full attention, always a powerful inducement for me to grin like an idiot. I slipped off my shoes under the table and let my stockinged feet rest atop his loafers.

"This whole thing is like you walk into an elevator and then you smell that someone, or maybe more than just one someone, has used the elevator as a *pissoir*. I don't want to stay in that elevator, but I don't want to lug my big suitcase up five flights to where I'm going either."

Thorne's mouth twitched into his barely noticeable smile.

"How do I come up with a clear-cut answer about whodunit when everything about this situation smells? Don's helmet strap — when I was riding my helmet, once it was strapped on, simply would not come off until I unsnapped it. There's a locking mechanism like a luggage strap under your chin and it takes finger pressure on both sides of the clasp to unlock it. Was Don's helmet messed with before the race? Hank's photos show that Jenny and Kyle were there, and that Kyle might have thrown something. I'm pretty sure Thalia lied about not being there on an ATV with something like a pellet gun in her hand. From the photo evidence, do we have enough to prove that the accident wasn't just an accident after all? I don't think so."

Both Thorne's eyebrows lifted and his head tilted a millimeter—his substitute for a confirming shrug.

"And although there's no evidence at all that Bryce the night nurse was in any way responsible when Don died in the wee hours while no one was watching, I'm wondering about that too. Because Jenny caught Bryce lying, and something about that guy makes me uneasy."

Thorne nodded along in an almost indiscernible way as I talked through these points.

"Do I ask Thalia who the investigating police detective is? Do I ask Jenny that? And hand over the photos to the detective? Just turn everything over to the powers that be and let it go? Do I make sure someone is staying with Mater at all times, just in case? And if Bryce shows up in her room do I ask him what he's doing away from his usual work location at the hospital?"

"Or E," Thorne said.

"All of the above?"

His infinitesimal smile twitched.

"Because asking the questions and keeping watch on Mater 24/7 may cause one or the other of those people to do something definitive, yes?"

He nodded again, but you'd need a micrometer to measure it.

"Okay then. Shall we head home and change? And then I'm going to start stirring the pot. I'll make the calls to Thalia and Jenny and then go see Mater. I'll give Collin and Lulu a break, and keep an eye out for Bryce."

Thorne stood up, and even though his movements were always as smooth as a panther's, every head in the restaurant turned to see what was causing the great disturbance in the Force. When he reached his full height all of them continued to gaze at him because, well, Thorne.

≈37≈

"Hi Thalia, it's Xana."

"I can't talk right now," she said. "I'm dealing with paperwork and insurance and all that crap."

"When would be a convenient time to talk, then? Because I tracked down the photographer at Cougar Rock and I'd like to show you some of the photos."

Silence.

"Thalia?"

"You did what?"

"We don't have to talk about this now, since you're busy. Just let me know when you might have some time available, or I can scan the photos and send them to you, if you'd prefer."

"Oh for Chrissake, why did you bother? I

mean, Don's gone. What difference does it make how he fell?"

"I think the police will care about how he fell, Thalia. And they'll care if there's proof of who was at Cougar Rock that day. I think they'll want to look at his helmet, too. What's the name of the detective who was investigating? And do you have his or her contact information?"

Silence.

"Would you like to give me your email? I can send you copies of the photos. It will save us both a trip. We can talk once you've had a chance to look at them."

"Yolanda said you would help me."

"I think it's more likely that Yolanda said I could read your cards, and that I was good at doing that."

Silence.

"Jenny and Kyle were there that day too. Could you give me Jenny's phone number? I'd like to give her the opportunity to see the photos as well."

Silence.

"Well, here's what I'll do then. I'll get your mailing address from Yolanda, and I'll see if I can track Jenny down and get her address as well. And I'll make copies of the photos and send you both a set. We can talk again once you've had a chance to look at what they show. How's that?"

"I can't believe you have pictures, or that they

show anything useful. And pictures can be doctored."

"I won't keep you, since you're busy. I'll get the photos in the mail to you right away. Thanks, Thalia."

I hung up before she could call me a name my mother would find declassée.

I tracked Jenny down by calling the horse barn, and the barn manager told me Jenny was there and she would bring her to the phone. I waited, wondering whether Jenny would take the call, but after a few minutes she said a grudging "Hello." I reminded her who I was and where we'd met, and then before she could say something privileged and arrogant I fired off another figurative flare.

"Jenny, I've got photographs from Cougar Rock on race day. You and Kyle are there."

"So? Of course we were there. We were riding with Don."

"I think you should take a look at the photos before I provide a set for the police."

"I thought you were Thalia's friend. Why would you give photos to the police that show what a liar she is?"

"Because the photos also show your son with his arm extended. As if he had thrown something toward Don. And I think it's possible someone damaged the strap on Don's helmet."

"No way."

"I'm afraid it's yes."

Silence.

"If you give me your address I'll mail them to you, or I can scan them and email them if you'd prefer."

She preferred email, but not before calling me one of those declassée words Mater decries.

ר   ר   ר

I wore linen slacks and a collared blouse to visit my Mom, because she believes denim is anathema unless you are digging a ditch or roping a calf.

I kissed Collin and Lulu hello, and also my resolutely incommunicado mother, and then kissed Collin and Lulu goodbye as they headed off to walk at the beach. They'd spent the last couple of days in the hospital room and who could blame them for wanting to get some exercise and breathe cool salty air as they strolled alongside the Pacific Ocean? Not me.

I took a quick jaunt down to the fourth floor to ask the Charge Nurse if Bryce was working. He wasn't, so I kissed my non-reciprocating Mater goodbye, drove home and tracked down my siblings at the beach.

≈38≈

Bryce couldn't help smiling. He'd maneuvered himself into position and was ready to act.

"They won't know what hit them. They think they're safe. I am so much smarter than those privileged dumbbells. They can't keep me from doing what I am here on earth to do."

He checked his pocket for the syringe.

Fentanyl this time. Less than two milligrams was all it would take, but he had squirreled away enough to fill the ten milliliter syringe. That much Fentanyl would bring down a herd of elephants, and the overdose symptoms would mimic a heart attack.

He slid his pinky into his ear. Nice and clean in there. Perfect.

≼34≽

After a long amble at Ocean Beach with Collin and Lulu I felt drawn back to the hospital. I've learned to heed these inexplicable urges or be sorry afterward, although I would probably be sorrier if heeding this one would mean empty hours of watching Mater refuse to communicate.

I checked the hallway as I approached to be sure the nurses and aides hadn't seen me. It was after visiting hours, but with critical care patients those hours are often relaxed for family members. I didn't want to find out that this hospital enforced a stricter visitor policy.

Instead of lying still and mute, Mater was sitting up and watching television. She clicked it off with a brisk thumb on the remote as soon as I walked into the room.

"Alexandra, don't leave me alone with him," she whispered, pointing at the doorway.

"Who?" We both whispered.

"Whom, dear."

"Mother, please."

"Oh, don't be ridiculous. You must listen to me, Alexandra. That awful nurse is here."

"What awful nurse? Wait. You mean the man from the fourth floor?"

"Yes. That one. I can't put my finger on what it is about him; he's just dreadful without my being able to pinpoint exactly why I think so. And Lulu and Collin won't listen to me about anything."

"His name is Bryce, right?"

"I haven't the faintest idea. I don't pay attention to the staff names. They come and they go all day, poking and prodding and making me get up and walk, and then they make me lie down and they reconnect me to all these machines."

"But Bryce is off-duty tonight. I asked downstairs."

"I asked him why he was here. He says he picked up a shift. He said this floor was short-handed tonight and he took the extra shift. 'Isn't that lucky for me?' he said, and then he smiled the strangest smile. He gives me the shivers."

"Me too, Mother."

I looked at her until she made eye contact.

"Mom, I will make sure that nothing happens

to you because of that nurse. Do you understand me?"

"How can you possibly...?"

"You know what I can do, Mother. You've seen me be capable in dangerous situations, and heaven knows how formidable you are. You and I are going to work as a team, okay? Together we'll be safe."

Mater narrowed her eyes for a moment. Then, maybe because she was wearing a cheap cotton gown, tied to a hospital bed by tubes, and far from her hairdresser and pedicurist and diamonds, Mater looked at me with what I believe was recognition. For the first time in my life Mater saw me for who I am and not as someone who had consistently failed to be what she wanted me to be.

Mater nodded and I took her hand and squeezed. She squeezed back.

I called Thorne. I am a grown-ass woman and more than capable of handling tough situations by myself, but Thorne is an order of magnitude tougher and grown-asser.

Also I believe that I am only an occasional idiot, and squaring off against a creepy guy who walks around with pocketsful of syringes loaded with who knows what poisonous drugs seemed a lot safer with Thorne-level back-up.

It turned out that having Thorne as my back-up didn't just *seem* safer.

=40=

Each tarot card reading I do for another person holds a lesson for me as well. Sitting in Mater's room waiting for Thorne I recalled Thalia's three-card layout: the Queen of Swords, the Hierophant reversed, and the Seven of Wands.

Mater was a widow like the Queen, and the Swords suit often intimates that someone is allowing his or her intellect to outweigh her unconscious and use language as a weapon instead of emotions as a connector. Had I used the threat of the photos as a weapon?

Hell yes.

As the Hierophant advises, though, I had been intent on listening to others as well as to my own inner voice, and now Mater was relying on her own intuition in spite of others' discrediting her gut reaction to Bryce.

In the reading the Hierophant was reversed, and his Hebrew letter, *Vav*, has a meaning: the nail. The Hierophant is not just about the traditions and religious beliefs that tie us together over history and bind us blindly or contentedly to dogma. He's about what connects us, or in his reversed state, separates us willfully from others, from our environment, our community, our spirit. He cautions us, when reversed, against shutting ourselves off from others and failing to listen to them and to our own soul's guidance. Was I fostering my connectedness to my friends? To my mother and family? To Thorne? To my zillion pets? To my own true self? I realized that my mother and I had connected over our concern for what Bryce might be capable of, and I was glad we had seen eye to eye for once.

The conflict characterized by the Seven of Wands card was no mystery; Thalia was in conflict with her husband, her kids, her husband's lover, herself (maybe), and now me. Jenny was clashing with Thalia and probably her husband, her kids, and now me. Mater was likely to be squabbling with the hospital staff, but for once not with me.

I was contending with Thalia and Jenny, trying to get to the truth that the Hierophant always demands of us. The truth is the standard he calls us to adhere to; he admonishes us that we always know the truth when we hear it, be it self-evident to our intellect or only to our internal monitors.

In the midst of all this adversity, the sweetest use I could put this experience to was to uncover the truth about Don's death and Nurse Bryce. I understood the Seven of Wands to represent the forces allied to prevent me from doing that.

Not just me, though. Thorne and my mother and me. We would be enough.

≈41≈

While we waited for Thorne, I checked my phone to see in what California County the Tevis Cup Race takes place and found that most of the trail appears to cross Placer County. Cougar Rock's jurisdiction, in the middle of the wilderness, is therefore likely to lie with the Placer County Sheriff rather than with a specific town's police department.

I searched the Placer County website and found the contact information for the Sheriff's Investigations Division, copying the link and mailing it to myself so that I could follow up with a phone call during office hours the next morning.

The next morning, however, I would be otherwise occupied.

≈42≈

Thorne glided silently into the room.

"Did he see you?" I asked.

Which was, of course, a nonsensical question. No one sees Thorne unless he wishes to be seen. I don't know how he pulls that one off, but he does. Because he thinks of everything, he'd brought homemade tortilla-wrapped turkey, bacon and avocado roll-ups for the night's vigil, and a thermos of iced tea for me.

"Thank God you're here," Mater said to him, stretching out her hand palm-down, as if she expected him to kiss it.

Thorne took her hand as if he were greeting a grand duchess and patted it with his other hand. Gazing into Thorne's eyes, Mater adopted the "I'm so helpless" expression I'd seen her wear with all her previous husbands. I reminded my-self that Mater has not yet had any psychotherapy and is sorely lacking in basic, non-manipulative communication skills.

"Mother, we're going to hide in the bathroom. If Bryce comes into the room alone and tries to use a syringe or does anything at all that you don't like, you yell my name as loud as you can. That's the plan, okay?"

"Can't Thorne just sit here by me? Bryce wouldn't dare..."

The room was dimly lit, but she was doing what looked a lot like batting her eyelashes at my mighty sweetie.

"Mother," I said, "We don't know how long you're going to be in this hospital. We can't spend every night for weeks on end keeping watch. And if Bryce is truly dangerous, he needs to be stopped. I think he may have killed my friend's husband, and who knows how many other pa-tients. So even if we keep him from harming you, I'm afraid he'll just harm someone else."

"I don't care if he harms someone else."

"Mother."

"Well, I don't."

Talk about uncovering the truth...

"Mother, Thorne and I agree that this is the smartest way to handle it."

"Is that right?" she asked him. Because what I say doesn't count.

Thorne turned to me. I raised my eyebrows in an imitation of his usual "Up to you, Babe."

"Yes," he said to my mother, in his voice that sounds like the guy who sang, "You're a Mean One, Mr. Grinch." Thorne's resonating basso and minimal verbiage carry all his conviction and integrity with them, so my mother sighed and resigned herself to the plan.

I required her to repeat what she should do, and that she should only do it if Bryce was alone and pulling out a syringe or fiddling with the machine that dosed her with medication.

ר   ר   ר

Thorne and I sat on the tan tile floor in the bathroom, our backs against the beige-painted wall. The floor radiated coldness upward. I slipped my arm under Thorne's and we interlaced fingers. I stopped feeling cold.

The bathroom smelled of bubble-gum air freshener and liquid soap. We were content to be with each other, quiet as we often were, not feeling any need to chat. We had a plan to execute, and chatting was irrelevant. We were waiting, which was enough.

I realized later that our holding hands allowed him to haul me to my feet before I could have risen on my own.

"Alexandra!"

Thorne was up and out of the bathroom door before Mater finished calling my name. Her voice was more of a hoarse cough than a shout, so I hesitated, wondering what was going on. But Thorne heard it for what it was and we catapulted out of the bathroom, Thorne in front, blocking my view.

I stepped to the side and saw Mater yanking her left arm across her body, the arm with the port into her metacarpal vein. She was clawing at the hand, her voice barely audible because she was terrified, trying to pull out the line that ran to her arm from the Pyxis machine.

"I fell asleep," she croaked. She yanked the medical tape and IV port out of her hand and blood ran down her fingers.

Bryce had his syringe poked into the IV port on the Pyxis, his thumb on the plunger. I couldn't tell if he'd managed to inject anything already, but Mater was safe for now. The shock on Bryce's face when he saw Thorne coming at him only lasted for a moment, but the shock kept his thumb from pressing down further.

Thorne bear-hugged a now snarling Bryce to pull him away from Mater's IV, and Bryce pulled the syringe away with him as he was lifted off the floor, his feet kicking at Thorne's shins. He twisted his lower arm toward Thorne's side, ready to jab with the syringe.

Thorne swiveled so Bryce's right hand and the syringe faced me, and I grabbed Bryce's wrist and forced his hand down to his side. Nurses are strong from shifting patients and equipment, but I was in that slowed-down, car-lifting adrenaline-powered state that would never permit Bryce to prevail.

The syringe's needle disappeared into the fabric covering Bryce's thigh and I put the weight of my entire body into the effort, shoving the syringe hard with my hip. I felt the needle resisting as it punctured the meat of his upper leg, and he and I stared straight at each other for a moment. He tilted his head as if asking a question.

Then Bryce pushed the plunger on the syringe and in another moment his lips turned blue and he seized, his body going stiff.

≈43≈

"Go," I said to Thorne. His off-the-grid status, with no ID, no bank account, no known address that he would care to reveal to hospital personnel or law enforcement, meant that he could not own any part of the actions that resulted in Bryce's death. He lowered Bryce to the floor and glided like a python from the room.

Mater was jabbing at the call button and calling for help in a frantic croak.

"Stop," I said, and took the button from her hand. "Everything is all right now. It's all over. You're safe."

I couldn't think of any more comforting clichés or I would have voiced them as well. Instead, I took her hand and said "Shhh. Shhh. Shhh."

A nurse came into the room and stopped short when she saw Bryce on the floor.

"He tried to kill my mother," I said. "Check the syringe. He was about to inject the syringe into her IV. My guess is it's an opioid."

The nurse stared. Then she walked over to Bryce and felt his carotid for a pulse. She pulled back an eyelid to check his blown cornea. When she saw that he was unresponsive she stood and said, "What the hell just happened here?"

"I told you. My bet is that my mother isn't the first patient he's targeted and killed. I'd recommend you use whatever antidote you have for opioid overdose, but he injected a massive amount, based on what I saw in the syringe."

She just stared at me, shocked into immobility.

"If you can't revive him, or even if you can, call whoever you call when there's been a problem like this. Start with whoever does hospital security at night, and then you should escalate to whoever handles administrative emergencies. At least that's what I would do if I were you. But I'm sure you have procedures."

"Stay here," the nurse said.

"I'm not going to leave my mother until you clean that mess up and she feels safe."

As soon as the nurse walked out, but before the army of medical and staff personnel invaded, I made sure Mater understood that Thorne had never been in her hospital room.

"They won't believe you did that all by your-self," Mater said.

"You're the only one who can tell them a different story," I said. "If you have the faintest flicker of gratitude you will not rat out your savior. Let me handle the questions, if you like. Play the trauma victim whose memory is unclear. You fell asleep, remember. Please do this for me and for Thorne, Mother."

She acquiesced, and she was splendid at acting oblivious, but I'm pretty sure she did it for Thorne rather than for me. I didn't care who she did it for as long as she grasped the need for it and did it.

The aftermath took all night. I was asked again and again to describe what happened. The Naxolone antidote the medical team administered multiple times failed to bring Bryce around. They tried to reinsert Mater's IV port in her hand, but she was having none of it, thank you, shoving her hand underneath herself in the bed. She wouldn't let them clean up the blood from the yanked IV; I did that for her.

"You need to preserve the evidence," I kept saying. "Check the IV port on my mother's machine. See if there isn't a non-prescribed opioid in there. If you don't do that immediately I'm going to call the police and make sure it gets done. He tried to kill my mother."

Finally one of the doctors took me seriously, and with his gloves on he removed the syringe from Bryce's leg.

"Are your fingerprints on this?" he asked me.

"No."

The story Mater and I stuck to was that once Bryce realized he was caught, he injected himself. I repeated the story of Bryce's strange behavior with another patient the previous week. Once the doctor returned and said Bryce's syringe had contained Fentanyl, and there was no charted prescription for it on Mater's record, they backed off with the accusations.

The police were never summoned. I think the hospital risk management team took a look at the list of patients who had died on Bryce's watch and decided to stonewall, in case that would reduce the number of wrongful death lawsuits.

I asked Mater for the name of her Pebble Beach doctor and, as daylight flooded her hospital room, I arranged for an ambulette to transfer her immediately to Monterey Community Hospital, just outside the Highway 1 gate to the 17-Mile Drive.

There was no objection by the St. Joseph medical or administrative personnel to transferring the patient.

≈44≈

I arrived back at the house in time for Collin
and Lulu to make me breakfast. I hadn't wanted
to wake them up in the middle of the night, so my
scrambled eggs were cold by the time the whole
story came out.

"Where is Captain Cold-Cock?" Collin said
when I had told them everything.

"Wherever he wants to be," I said. "And
watch it with the cock references."

Collin smiled.

"We need to thank him," Lulu said. "Or is he
like the Lone Ranger, leaving before anyone can
say thank you?"

"Pretty much," I said. "But he likes homemade baked goods."

Lulu and Collin drove away, headed to Monterey to meet up with Mater at the community hospital. Collin would say goodbye to Mater and continue on to Los Angeles; Lulu was local, so she would take responsibility for keeping watch over Mater and baking carrot cake muffins for Thorne.

I reminded them that while at the Monterey hospital they were not to discuss with Mater Thorne's involvement in any events of the previous hospital stay. No telling who might be listening.

The house empty and the dishes in the machine washing, I let the dogs out to the side yard dog run, gave them a biscuit when they returned, fed the kitties, and went upstairs to my bed.

I wanted to take a shower but the adrenaline had worn off, the food-triggered torpor had kicked in, and I was afraid I would fall asleep standing up. I barely got my shoes off in time to fall over onto the cool sheets and fade out.

≋45≋

I faded in, not long enough later, when the doorbell rang.

I ignored it. The dogs didn't, barking their alarm and barreling downstairs to the front door.

The doorbell rang again, a long push that raised a steady b-r-r-r-ing. Whoever was pressing the bell nonstop did not mean to be ignored.

I crossed the upstairs hall to the front bedroom that I use for an office and opened the window.

"Who is it?" I called down.

"Open the door, Xana. I came to pick up those pictures."

Thalia, this time in black yoga pants and a violet tank top, wanted to come in. But I have a history with antagonistic people who want to enter my home and I had no interest in extending that history into the present.

"Just a sec," I said.

I grabbed a manila envelope from the station-ery shelves. Downstairs in the dining room I picked up a set of photos and slid them into the envelope, threading the metal clasp through the flap's hole and pushing the clasp's wings to the side to keep the flap closed.

Back upstairs I went. I opened the window.

"Here you go," I called, and dropped the en-velope.

Thalia ducked her head and then chased the envelope to where it had floated back and forth to the sidewalk a few feet away. She picked it up and shook it at me.

"Wait. That's it? You're not going to let me in?"

"Nope. I've had a long night, and you woke me up. I'm going back to sleep. As for the photos, you're welcome."

"Who was the photographer, then? I saw a guy with gray hair and a plaid shirt that day. Was that him? Zipping shut all his camera cases when the helicopter showed up?"

"No, Thalia. You can't make this information disappear. And you just admitted that you were there at Cougar Rock after denying it multiple times to me."

A smallish red SUV pulled up to the curb,

blocking my driveway. Blocking a driveway in San Francisco is a cardinal sin even the Pope can't absolve you from, no matter how regretfully you confess your error and drop large bills into the poor box.

"Uh oh," I said, pointing.

Thalia, whose ears were already emitting tiny jets of steam, instantly lost her shit.

Jenny climbed out of her car and the two women exchanged vituperation at some length. While that was going on, I grabbed another manila envelope and repeated the process of loading it with a set of photos.

"Hey Jenny! This is your set!" I called down to her, but I don't believe she heard me over the combined screeching, nor did she make any move to pick up the envelope where it lay.

I did not care to listen to what was going on between the women. One or the other or both were the cause of Don's death, which he did not deserve no matter how big a cheating fuckwit he was. The post-mortem rivals were creating a public nuisance, so I called the cops on them. I wasn't the only one. It seems my neighbors were disturbed by the ruckus, which had escalated into hair- pulling and handbag-swinging.

While I waited for law enforcement to arrive, I washed my face and put on clean clothes in an effort to feign consciousness when they showed up, which was promptly. Two cars.

I let the first two officers, a man and a woman, into the house after they managed to separate the women and get them seated, one each, in the back of their squad cars. I gave the third set of photos to them, explaining the nature of the pictures. I aimed the cops' follow-up at the Placer County Sheriff.

Jenny's car was still blocking my driveway and the policewoman offered to let me move Jenny's car if Jenny would let me have the keys, but Jenny used some declassée terminology for me at that point, so no go. The cop called for more backup and a tow and eventually Jenny's car rolled away, its front end hanging up in the air, behind a big yellow truck.

Jenny and Thalia refused to stop their scrapping and they wound up rocking back and forth, yelling and handcuffed on their way to a date with the San Francisco criminal justice system.

≈*46*≈

I was too wired to go back to sleep, so I called my sister Nora and brought her up to date. She said she and the kids would make a day trip to Monterey on Saturday to see Mater and take the 17-Mile Drive, followed by afternoon ice cream in Carmel and dinner at Auntie Lulu's.

I called Thorne to see how he felt about lunch at the East-West Café. He felt good about it. Not because he said so, but because he materialized, car keys in hand, in the garage doorway at the bottom of my front steps.

Today's special was "Adobo with Rise Pill Off," which sounded great, so we ordered some and it was.

≈47≈

I followed up with the Placer County Sheriff's office after calling Hank Jessen to let him know the Sheriff would likely be in touch about the photos.

The story made the local news because the Tevis Cup is a big deal. The Placer County District Attorney had trouble creating any sort of provable case against anyone and had to let the murder go unprosecuted. Yes, Kyle threw a stone at the horse. Yes, Thalia shot a pellet at the horse. Yes, the strap on the helmet showed evidence of tampering.

But also yes, the footing on the trail at Cougar Rock is treacherous, and Buddy may have reared and skidded on his own, since Arab horses are notorious for responding to the slightest unanticipated stimulus by jittering around as if they're high on crack. Once Don was in the hospital Bryce may have injected him with an overdose, but Bryce and the syringe were both gone. So who was directly responsible for Don's death?

When I asked my inner voice for an answer, the response was, "All of them."

I wondered if an autopsy on Don might reveal the overwhelming presence of opioids, but I remembered that, contrary to Greek Orthodox tradition, Thalia had had Don cremated once the hospital had extracted any organs they could use.

"I'm not paying to bury that jerk," is how she'd put it. "I'll take his ashes to the dump and scatter them."

I was frustrated that there would be no clear resolution, no court case, no "justice," but life is messy and sometimes there is no justice. I think learning to accept the lack of "closure," the messiness of life, is our job as adults.

And who knows what effect Don's death would have on those who had contributed to it? I don't believe anyone can pave over their consciousness of having committed murder. I thought of Lady Macbeth, scrubbing imaginary blood from her hands.

I also think Shakespeare was being both sardonic and honest when he wrote that there was sweetness in adversity. Adversity is brutal and disturbing, anything but sweet, but with any luck we learn and grow, becoming better, wiser human beings from the lessons our sufferings teach us.

≈48≈

Thorne wore a lightweight wool-blend gray suit, white dress shirt and royal blue tie to DeDe's wedding. I put on a aqua linen shift and high heels, because at the reception I wanted to dance with Thorne and not have it look like Chewbacca was waltzing with a Munchkin.

Just to annoy Mater, who was finally out of the hospital and crabby about no longer being allowed to eat bacon cheeseburgers, I asked the usher to seat us on the groom's side at the chapel.

DeDe was glowing in a shell pink Alençon lace overblouse and calf-length duchesse satin skirt as she walked toward the altar past the standing congregants. Her oldest son escorted her. Bix's face when he caught sight of DeDe reddened, and he pulled a handkerchief out of his pocket to dab at his eyes.

Exactly how you want a wedding to be.

At the reception Thorne and I waltzed as if it were still the Nineteenth century. Yes of course he can ballroom dance. My titanic twinkletoes.

≋49≋

DeLeon, Maxine, Nora, Nora's husband Hal, and Yolanda and her boyfriend LaKeith were having potluck with us. Thorne grilled steaks, Maxine brought garlic bread and sweet potato pie, YoYo her mac and cheese of course, and Nora brought a zucchini, tomato and onion casserole.

I opened bags of baby lettuce and baby spinach, threw the contents into a big wooden bowl, heaved a basket of cherry tomatoes on top, tossed the result with some house-made herb vinaigrette dressing I had spirited home from the East/West Café, and allowed as how my work was done here.

Oh, wait; I also set the table. Please hold your applause.

Thorne and I sat on the deck looking out over

the marine layer floating like miles of soft gray dryer lint atop the dark ocean. I was curled up on Thorne's lap because the evening was chilly, not to say frigid, the way it tends to be in August in San Francisco. DeLeon sat wearing his nylon parka in the chair next to Thorne's. The dogs were outside with us, in the cold but away from the food, and the cats, having none of any of it, were upstairs under a bed. The remainder of our guests drank wine inside and caught up with each other around the kitchen island.

"That Hierophant card," I said. "He's all about finding your own spiritual truth."

Thorne pulled me in a little closer.

"He tells us to listen for the truth, and to do that we have to listen to our own guides, and assess our gut reaction to what other people tell us. We have to respect everyone's right to his or her own true nature. And we can't listen or assess without being willing to forge a connection, empathy, with the other person."

"Why I'm here," Thorne said.

"Why I'm here too," DeLeon said.

"Because I connect with you gentlemen. We-all's got empathy."

"Believe that," DeLeon said.

Thorne nodded, but I don't think DeLeon could have seen it. I only knew about the nod because I could feel Thorne's head shift minutely.

To Thorne, I said "I see people get stuck on

the physicality of you, the intimidating bulk, and they don't look past that."

He nodded.

"You also enjoy that reaction, and take advantage of it in your work."

He smiled his miniscule smile.

"DeLeon, you just like surprising people," I said.

"The shockingly well-educated and erudite African," he said, using his Oxford don pronunciation for a moment. "But Ms. Yolanda is servin' her mac and cheese in there, and I'm gonna get mine before it's gone, because baby girl I am no fool," DeLeon said, standing and opening the French doors.

He blocked Hawk and Kinsey from following him inside, and they sat down to stare through the doors at the food being carried to the dining room table by my family and friends. Where the dogs' noses pressed against the doors plumes of exhalation spread out onto the glass.

I'd purchased lemon bars especially for DeLeon and I thought he might skip the entrées and go straight to his dessert, shielding the entire batch from grabby hands.

Yolanda had brought a second tray of mac and cheese and it was hidden in Thorne's downstairs fridge, so I saw no need to hurry inside for dinner. I could hear my sister Nora laughing at something YoYo said.

"I wish people wouldn't lie," I said to Thorne. "It tears at the fabric of our connections to each other. And all you have to do is see one of the Earth photos from the space station and you realize we're all in this thing together. We are all connected whether we want to be or not. Why would anyone want to damage our need for each other?"

He shook his head in a tiny acknowledgement of the folly of the human condition.

"I should stop talking now, huh? We should join the others."

He lifted his eyebrows in a "Whatever you want, Babe" response.

What I wanted to do was kiss him, so I did, on his miniscule smile.

Bevan Atkinson, author of *The Tarot Mysteries*, including *The Fool Card*, *The Magician Card*, *The High Priestess Card*, *The Empress Card*, *The Emperor Card*, and *The Hierophant Card*, lives in the San Francisco Bay Area and is a long-time tarot card reader.

Bevan currently has no pets but will always miss Sweetface, the best, smartest, funniest dog who ever lived, although not everyone agrees with Bevan about that.